Valley of Zin

a culinary mystery introducing
Josephine St. John

written and illustrated by

Geraldine Duncann

Vintage Press
Sonoma, California

Valley of Zin

Text and illustrations Copyright © 2007 by

Geraldine Duncann

ISBN: 978-0-932824-24-0
Printed in the United States of America

Vintage Press
Sonoma, California

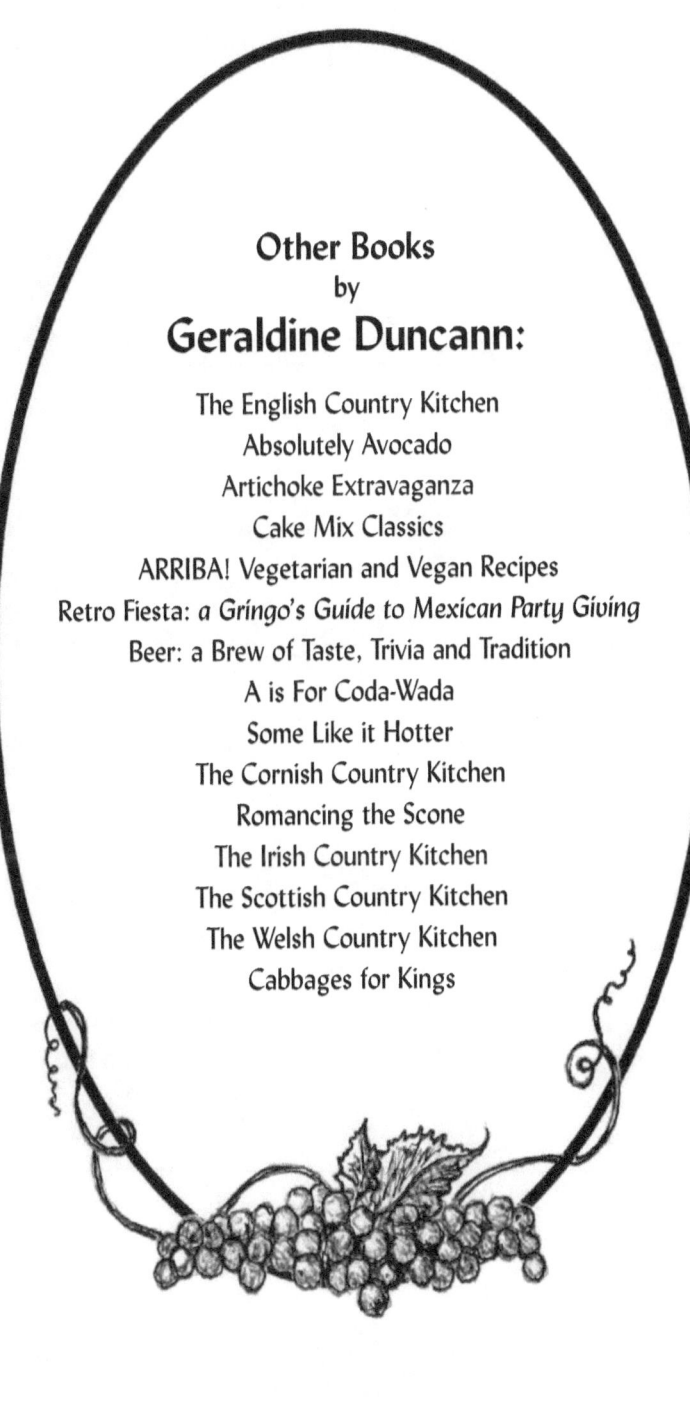

Other Books
by
Geraldine Duncann:

The English Country Kitchen
Absolutely Avocado
Artichoke Extravaganza
Cake Mix Classics
ARRIBA! Vegetarian and Vegan Recipes
Retro Fiesta: *a Gringo's Guide to Mexican Party Giving*
Beer: a Brew of Taste, Trivia and Tradition
A is For Coda-Wada
Some Like it Hotter
The Cornish Country Kitchen
Romancing the Scone
The Irish Country Kitchen
The Scottish Country Kitchen
The Welsh Country Kitchen
Cabbages for Kings

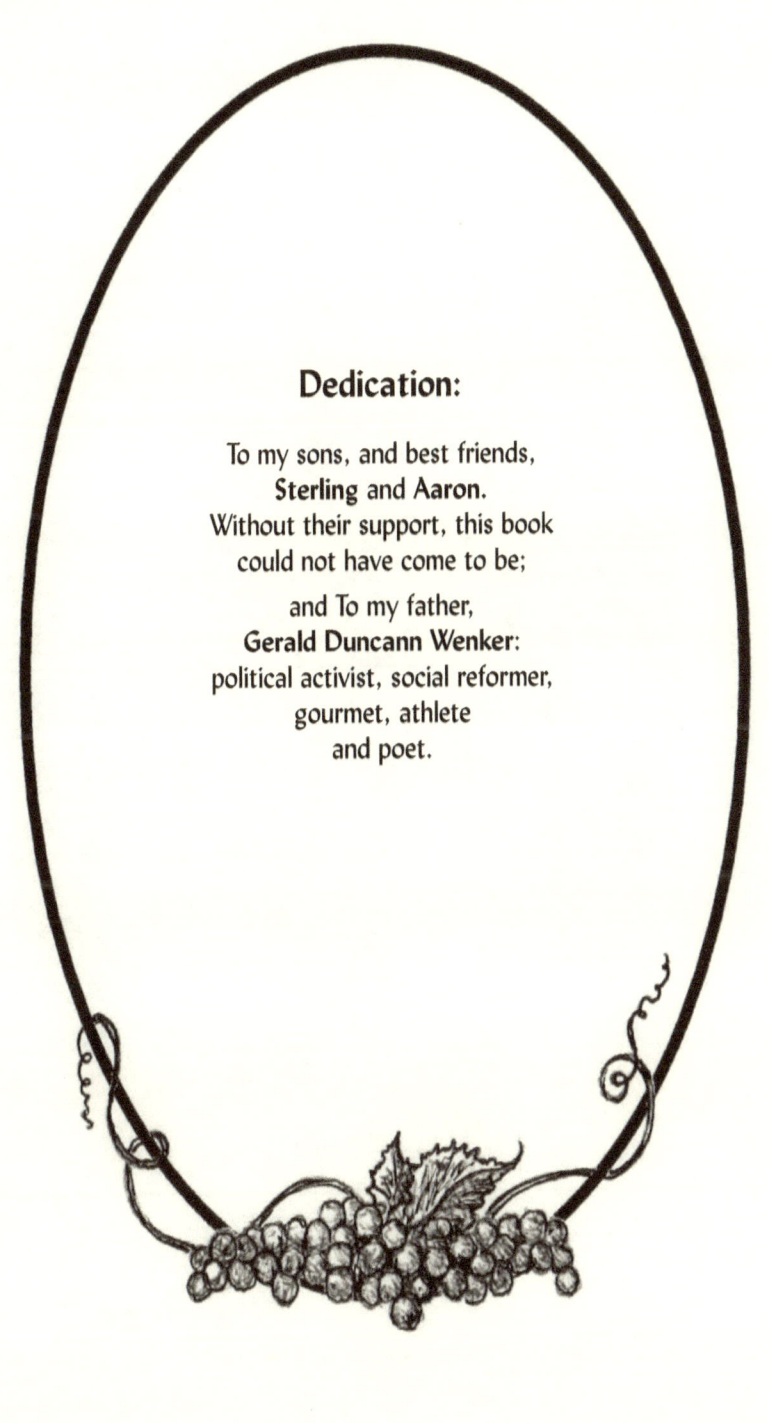

Dedication:

To my sons, and best friends,
Sterling and **Aaron**.
Without their support, this book
could not have come to be;

and To my father,
Gerald Duncann Wenker:
political activist, social reformer,
gourmet, athlete
and poet.

Acknowledgments:

My thanks goes to my editor Judy Agard,
who managed to turn my spelling and
punctuation into something resembling the
English language, and to my close friends
Henry Partridge and Janice Cullum, who aided in
this process;

to my son Sterling and my close friend Asa, who with
patience, persistence and fortitude helped this aged
technophobe with the ongoing process of becoming one with
a cantankerous computer;

to all my friends in the Sonoma county wine community,
particularly the accommodating, friendly and knowledgeable
people at Sunce and Taft Street Wineries for answering
numerous questions;

and to Hoyt Smith, Betsy O'Connor and Dianne Nicolini of
KDFC radio who made the hours I spent chained to my
desk a bit less tedious, with glorious music and their
delicious wit.

to Marshall Fenstermaker for technical
information about firearms

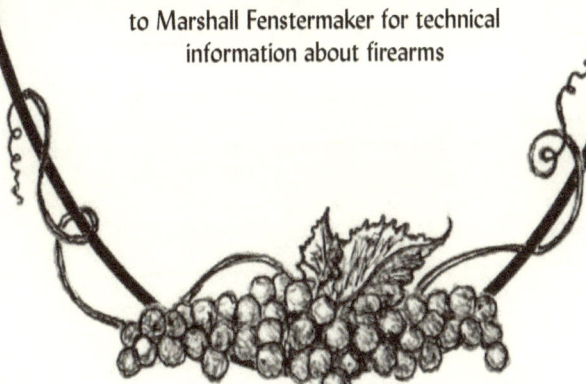

Introduction

This book is the biographical account of an episode in the life of food, wine and travel writer Josephine St. John. The characters are fictitious and any similarity to persons living or dead is purely accidental with the exception of references to historical figures. In the book, I have taken the liberty of having Father Sean O'Malley be a descendant of the Vallejo/Haraszthy dynasty of Sonoma vintners. This is complete fabrication. Two of the sons of Agoston Haraszthy did indeed marry two of the daughters of Mariano Vallejo, and there are descendants of that union still living in the Sonoma valley and still involved in the wine industry, however my character, Father Sean and his family are pure fiction. For more information about Haraszthy and Vallejo, other tidbits of Sonoma history and some interesting travel tips, see Jo's notes in the back of the book. The old Mountain Cemetery does exist and visitors are welcome. General Vallejo, some of the descendants of Haraszthy and some of the Sebastian's of wine making fame, are buried there along with others who played significant roles in the history of Sonoma, the California wine industry and the history of California herself. Jo's favorite cafe in downtown Sonoma does not exist. The building, The Blue Wing Inn, however does, and is on the national register of historic places. It is directly across Spain Street from the old mission. It is one of the oldest adobe buildings in Northern California and housed the first hotel north of San Francisco. Some people of note who stayed there include Ulysses S. Grant, John Fremont, "Fighting" Joe Hooker, (of Civil War fame) William T. Sherman and Phil Sheridan.

It is currently a private home and they would thank you to respect their privacy. If it were a cafe the upstairs veranda would indeed make a wonderful place sit with a glass of wine and watch the world go by. I have placed Jo's father in law, Ben Penella's vineyards on the on the Western side of Arnold Road. The O'Malley vineyards are to the North of him and the Gardino's to the South. You won't be able to find the actual locations from the maps provided, because the precise locations don't exist. I didn't think the actual residents and vintners, including my granddaughter and her family, would be pleased if curiosity seekers were to drive up and down their quiet country roads. The Jack London Ranch and London Ranch Road, in Glenn Ellen, do exist. Jack London Ranch is part o the California State Park System and open to the public. I hope you will enjoy Jo's recipes. Some are those she included in her Zinfandel cookbook. Others are just favorites of her family and friends. These are valid recipes because after all, I too am the author of cookbooks.

Geraldine Duncann, Sonoma – 2007
Your Vineyard or Mine

Prologue

It wasn't the rain that woke old Harry up, it was something else. Voices? Yes, it was voices. Angry voices. He peered out from under the protecting overhang of the old stone. He couldn't quite make anything out, but he thought he saw figures in the distance among the tomb stones. Ghosts, he thought. Well, why not? He'd seen them often enough before. He took a swig from his bottle of cheap port, pulled his tarpaulin back over himself, and tried to sleep.

"You know it's your baby!" Her hair was matted to her head by the warm autumn rain and her breasts showed through the water-soaked tee-shirt.

"How the hell could I possibly know that? You've spread your legs for every guy in Sonoma!" The rain splattered on the tombstones and ran in rivulets down the steep and rutted paths of the old cemetery.

"I have not! You know how much I love you. None of the others meant anything to me. I only love you and you know it." She blew droplets of rain off the end of her nose.

"That's damn hard to believe. You rub up to anyone who'll spend a few bucks on you. Jesus Christ! You know what they say about you?" He took a long pull from the beer he was holding. "They say you're like a bitch in heat with a pack of mongrels sniffing at your ass."

"What? That's a lie! It's not fair! I do not! Anyway, a girl has to have a little fun." She started to cry.

"A little fun, shit. You've fucked half the grape pickers in the county. That kid, if you are pregnant, could be anyone's. It'll probably pop out with a burrito in one hand and wearin' a sombrero. Go try to sucker someone else 'cause I ain't buyin' it."

"I am pregnant and it's yours. You know it is! And if you don't marry me, I'll tell everyone in town! I'll tell your father," she screamed. "I love you! You have to marry me!"

"You don't love me. You love my father's wallet, and if you think I'm going to let you give my family's name to some God-damned half-breed wetback, you've got another think coming. Me, marry trash like you? Shit! I'd rather marry a maggot!"

"Oooooh!" She flew at him, her hands formed into ridged talons. Before he could protect himself she managed to rake deep furrows down his left cheek, barely missing his eye. Blood welled up and spread into the rainwater running down his face. He wiped his cheek with the back of his hand and looked at it.

"You fucking cunt!" he yelled and gave her a backhand that sent her reeling. Losing her footing on the mossy stones, she stumbled and fell against a tombstone in the next plot. She lay still and silent. Everything was silent except for the rain and an owl. "Come on. Get the fuck up. I didn't hit you that hard...God damn it! Get up! Stop screwing around. Come on. Get up. I'll take you home. It's getting damn cold. We can talk about this tomorrow. Get up, God damn it!"

"Didn't know ghosts fought with each other," old Harry thought to himself as he took another pull from his bottle. It was raining harder now.

Chapter 1

The deep flavor lingered as I gazed out my office window instead of at my computer screen. Gawd, how I love Zinfandel: big, bold, brambly Zins that have been left on the oak for a long time. You can keep your thin, wimpy little Zins. They're a waste of a noble grape. A classic old-growth Zin's a wine that celebrates the harvest and comforts you in winter. Those little Zins; nice in a picnic basket in summer. But it's autumn now. Autumn in Sonoma, a glorious time of year. The gentle hills roll away to the horizon, sporting row after row of golden, amber and scarlet vines, their leaves crisping in the brusque autumn air. And even that air seems to glow with the quality of burnished old gold. Who am I to wax poetic about a glass of wine? Josephine St. John at your service. I'm a food and travel writer living in glorious Sonoma County, surrounded by some of California's most prestigious vines. I live with Lee, Jay, and Ben, two cats, three dogs, a rather large and useless black horse, two far more useful goats, assorted poultry and rabbits and the occasional pig or steer slated for the freezer. Bees. Ben also keeps bees. He says they help the grapes and olives. And yes, Ben grows, harvests, and cures olives in addition to his vineyards and winery. Ben retire? Not bloody likely. Lee and Jay are my two mostly adult sons and Ben is my father-in law.

Eighteen years ago, my husband, a brilliant man who had achieved numerous degrees from the University of California, brilliantly pitched himself off the north face of Half Dome in a climbing accident, leaving me with a house full of termites and two

3

infants. Ben, his father, insisted that we leave our Berkeley home and move in with him. Believe me, it didn't take much coaxing. His holdings consist of fifty acres of vineyards, a large Victorian farm house, the barns and winery, a pond and a stream. He dotes on the boys and they on him.

Having lived in this rather idyllic rural setting for the past eighteen years, I would now have a very hard time moving back into an urban situation. I would also have a hard time living in a contemporary house. They aren't built for people, they are built to maximize the contractors' profits. I like houses with molding around the windows and doors. I like houses with overhead lights in every room. I like houses with wood sash windows. Old houses have several things that I find essential: a cellar for storing all the canned fruit and pickles, jams, jellies and preserves you have made. O.K., I know. No one puts up their own fruit and pickles or makes their jams, jellies and preserves any more. I need a house with a service porch with laundry tubs. Without laundry tubs how can you wash large blankets and quilts, soak a dirty pair of Levis, wash off a pair of muddy boots or gut fish? You don't wash big old quilts or muddy boots or gut fish? Hmm. Imagine that. I need a house with a walk-in pantry to store fifty-pound sacks of flour, rice and beans. I need to be able to store all my herbs and spices; my jars of raisins and nuts, jars of Ben's honey, sacks of potatoes and ropes of garlic and onions. All right, so most of you don't buy your flour, beans and rice in fifty pound bags and your spices come in little two ounce cans. I know. I march to a different drummer. And I like a house with big, old, claw-foot bathtubs. Don't tell me you don't like to relax in a big old claw-foot tub full of bubbles now and then.

Now, don't get me wrong. I also want my house to have gushing torrents of piping hot water, be easily heated in winter, have an automatic washer and flush toilets. I'm not so old-fashioned that I don't want flush toilets, although I am quite capable of coping with the occasional plumbingless camping trip. Anyway, enough. Let's just say that Ben's old family home suits me just fine. Let me just add that one of the nicest features of this house is the large front veranda that faces the duck pond and meadow. Most mornings we can see deer drinking from the pond and grazing in the meadow.

Although both boys are studying music, they also have a passion for the wine business and fortunately, for machinery as well. Why is their passion for machinery fortunate? Ben has not updated the equipment in his small winery for decades. Most adolescent males can be found tinkering with a car. My two, and their grandfather, will most likely be found wrestling with the antiquated bottling machine or wine press; and of course, the occasional vehicle, since most of the vehicles on the property are relics as well.

Ben's holdings are small compared to both our neighbors. To one side of us are the O'Malley's. Despite the Irish name, they are one of the oldest families in the valley. The story goes that sometime in the late 1880's, Irish immigrant Sean O'Malley arrived in California and married into the Haraszthy-Vallejo clan of California wine legend. Father Sean Agoston Marina O'Malley is the oldest but chose to take the cloth, and so his sister, Deirdre Otelia Benicia O'Malley manages the estate and winery. Although our family is not of the Roman faith, Father Sean has been a very close friend and of great solace to me over the years.

The O'Malley holdings are large but nothing compared to the Gardinos who own all the land on the other side of us, and just about everything else Rodney Gardino Sr. can get his hands on. They are considered by the old-timers in the valley to be "upstart newcomers." Rod Sr. made his original pile in the stock market, or banking, or something (it's rumored he has mob connections) and when he moved to the valley in the 70's he began buying out a lot of the smaller vintners. He now has thousands of acres of vines scattered throughout both Sonoma and Napa Valleys. He doesn't make wine. He sells wine grapes to large producers. He also buys bulk wine and bottles it. With slick packaging and advertising he has made several fortunes, but the product is definitely mediocre.

Me, I don't make wine. I drink it, cook with it and write about it and that's what I was doing at the moment; writing a cookbook about Zinfandel. My deadline was fast approaching and I'm afraid I must confess to having spent far more time doing the research than in writing down the results thereof. Tonight, more research. I had invited friends over for dinner and to glean their opinions on several of the recipes I intended to include in the article. That was this evening. This afternoon I should be writing, not gazing out the window.

The rains had held off until last night, and the harvest was fortunately nearly finished. Ben should have a good year. Everyday he's out, walking among the vines, chuckling to himself as he peers into the little glass thing that measures the sugar content of the grapes. "We'll pick that south five acres tomorrow," he'd say, or "Nope, we'll let those go for another day or two." Then he'd glance appraisingly at the sky. "It won't rain before then," and so it went until all the grapes were in. Then he'd start on the olives.

"Mom! Grump, (my kids had called him Grump when they were little and it stuck) wants to know if you need me to bring up any more wine for dinner tonight."

"A few more bottles won't hurt. You know how Father Sean loves Grump's Zinfandel."

"Will do then. Can I have one of these little pastry things?"

"Sure, but just one. They're for tonight. Do you know where Lee is?"

"He and Alberto drove over to the feed store. Grump sent them to pick up a load of hay. Don't know why we keep Cindy any more. She can't do anything but eat."

"You know you'd miss that ol' nag as much as any of the rest of us if she was gone. You learned to ride on her. After what you guys put her through when you were kids, she deserves a pampered retirement." And that's just what Cindy was, a retired horse. I expected to see her sitting in the shade with a glass of sherry and an Agatha Christy novel. "Put the wine in the dining room when you bring it up. Don't forget to dust if off first," I yelled over my shoulder as I heard him open the kitchen door to the cellar. I glanced at the clock. Hell's bells! Three thirty already. I'd best get into the kitchen.

This was going to be a smallish dinner party, just the family, Father Sean, Allen Younger and Charley Archer (Charley incidentally is a woman) and Rossini Beryl Collin-Bennett, all people whose taste buds I respected. I usually try my recipes out on a few people whom I know will give me an honest opinion before sending them off to the publisher.

I had invited Lacey Coleman at the last minute. She was relatively new in town; came from someplace in the east and was currently in the process of opening an Art Gallery in Sonoma. I liked her and thought it would be good for her to meet some of the old timers. Besides, any group can use a bit of new blood now and then.

The menu was planned. Although some of the dishes did not sport Zinfandel, Zin enhanced dishes were the main emphasis and the reason for doing the dinner. We would begin with a few starters served around the fireplace before dinner. These would include a terrine liberally laced with Zinfandel and brandy, and the cheese tarts, if there were any left. At table we would begin with a soup of fresh beef broth enhanced with fresh mushrooms and Zinfandel. Because I needed feedback, the dinner was to feature two entrees, beef medallions in a Zinfandel reduction and a dish Jay had dubbed "Coq au Zin," a Zinfandel version on the classic French Coq au Vin, served with fresh hand-made pasta. Vegetables would include carrots in a Zinfandel glaze and fresh broccoli from the garden with freshly grated parmesan, no Zinfandel. All this would be accompanied by a salad of fresh greens, apples and walnuts with Zinfandel/cranberry vinaigrette. I make very good bread; a meal like this however, needs the excellent sourdough baguettes made by the Basque Boulangerie on the Plaza in downtown Sonoma. For dessert, I planned a light invention of mine that is not terribly sweet; perfectly ripened pear halves cored and placed on a bed of Escarole. These would then be filled with crumbled blue cheese with a bit of Zinfandel Port drizzled over the top and finished with a grinding of black pepper; light, elegant and a perfect accompaniment to the rest of the meal.

O.K. So I knew what I was going to cook and the groceries all assembled. Nonetheless, it still always takes me a bit of time to be able to kick into high gear so I took a basket and a pair of small sheers and went into the herb garden. I love my herb garden. Not only does it enhance my cooking, I love working in it. I love the smell when I brush against the fragrant leaves. I love the busy hum of the bees that are attracted to it and the butterflies that flit from plant to plant like bits of colored tissue paper.

These days most reputable markets carry a decent selection of fresh herbs. Growing my own is not necessary; my herb garden however, offers me a joy I cannot find in the market, particularly now that Ben and the boys have finally built an attractive and deer proof fence around it. Deer patrol was supposed to be the duty of Ben's dogs. Yeah! Right! Lazy mutts. The deer just step over them as they snooze. There wasn't an airplane however, that would dare to land on our property. The three of them went berserk whenever a plane passed overhead. Fortunately we weren't on a major flight path.

I gathered fresh chives, parsley and dill for the pasta, rosemary and sage for the chicken; some shallots for the beef medallions, a bit of fennel for the salad and then gathered some fresh flowers. On the way in I snapped off a small branch of fresh leaves from the California Bay Laurel tree which overhung the service porch. I greatly prefer my own fresh California bay to the dry Mediterranean variety.

Standing on the back stoop for a minute, I gazed out across the vines before returning to the kitchen and plunging head long into dinner preparations. Damn! Two more of the little cheese tartlets were gone. Jay! Damn it! I told you those tarts were for dinner tonight!"

"I only took one Ma! Honest! Must have been Grump."

"Don't call me Ma!"

"That's right. Blame everything on the old man," Ben's voice came from the pantry. "Anyway, as head of the household it's my duty to test anything guests are going to eat."

"Well, did they pass?"

"They'll do."

"They'll do! Is that all?" and I gave him a playful snap of a dishtowel as he emerged from the pantry.

"Hey! Ouch! That's elder abuse." He yelped, then with a sly grin, "Well, a bit better than 'they'll do'," and he quickly palmed another tart as he made for the back door. This time my dishtowel missed and knocked down the calendar instead.

"Damn!"

"Serves you right," he said sticking his head around the door and then quickly vanishing. Ben has a face like a prune, a body like Santa Claus and a mind like the proverbial steel trap. He's pushing eighty with a short stick and displays absolutely no sign of slowing down. He walks and tends his vines; he rides the old nag Cindy, though she complains bitterly, harvests and cures his olives, tends his bees and occasionally, if the boys are gone, milks the goats. He also tries to tell me how to cook! Oh yes, he's president of the local branch for Democratic reform, active in Greenpeace and gets himself to as many liberal/radical demonstrations as possible. He's constantly chiding me for what he considers my lack of political involvement. Ben reinforces my theory that an enthusiastic participation in life keeps you from falling apart sometime after forty.

Ben loves his land and what grows and lives on it. He loves his days and he loves his dogs. They are his constant companions, loping along ahead of him as he tends his vines and inspects his olive trees. Well, I couldn't really say that little Alistair lopes. On his tiny terrier legs, he trots double time, trying to keep pace with George, an English bulldog and Maggie. Maggie was the result of the misguided amour of a neighbors Russian Wolf Hound for a wandering St. Bernard. The result was a gargantuan, lovable mop who frequently knocks guests down with no malice. She just loves people and has no concept of her impact.

Now; it is important to know that Alistair, George and Maggie did not dislike Marmalade and Fritz. In fact quite the opposite. Woe be it to the intruder whom they perceived to be a threat to "their" cats. You could often find all five animals curled up together in front to the fire or exploring in the garden. The dogs did however, consider themselves self appointed disciplinarians. Heaven help the unwary feline caught in the act of trying to purloin a tidbit from the kitchen table.

Chapter 2

By five-thirty, my work in the kitchen was mostly done; the soup was finished, the chicken was tender perfection, the vegetables prepped and awaiting their finishing touches, the dough for the pasta resting and the reduction for the beef medallions awaiting a final dollop of butter. I just had to sear the beef and serve it up in its tasty sauce. The undressed salad was crisping in the fridge. Dessert had to be assembled at the time of serving.

The hors d'oeuvres were ready; one tray containing Ben's olives, my roasted, marinated red peppers, marinated mushrooms and the precious few remaining cheese tartlets. Another plate held the terrine accompanied by homemade black bread to spread it on, little green onions and fresh radishes from the garden. Ben and the boys would keep people entertained, passing the starters and pouring wine while I was in the kitchen putting the final touches on the meal.

I went upstairs to shower and dress. This little ritual always had a soothing effect and helped me change gears from harried kitchen staff to calm hostess. I wished Lee would get home.

Refreshed and relaxed, there was still half an hour before our guests arrived, I entered the kitchen only to find Marmalade and Fritz on the counter helping themselves to the terrine and the few remaining tartlets. "Scram you blasted marauding reivers," I shouted, and clapped my hands. That was a mistake for unfortunately Ben chose that moment to enter the kitchen with Alistair, George and Maggie, our self-appointed kitchen guards.

Immediately they leapt into action. George let forth with an earsplitting cacophony, more like a human being disemboweled than a dog barking. This of course sent Marmalade and Fritz several feet straight into the air and the tray with the remaining cheese tarts flying as well. Maggie was across the room in one gigantic bound, front paws landing on the counter, sending the plate with the terrine skidding across the counter and onto the floor. Alistair chased his own tail round and round in a circle, yapping furiously until he spotted the splattered terrine. He was extremely grateful for this legacy and showed his appreciation by setting too with great gusto, determined to not allow any of this delicious windfall to go to waste.

Fritz and Marmalade who had become twice their size managed to go through the cat door simultaneously with Maggie in hot pursuit but all she could ever manage to get through the small opening was her snout. Realizing she could not continue the chase, she returned to the kitchen to help George and Alistair clean the floor. In what seemed like seconds there wasn't a scrap of the terrine nor a single cheese tartlet to be seen. Maggie wallowed something about in her mouth thoughtfully, then spat an olive onto the floor and went to stand by the door, patiently waiting to be let out. George and Alistair gave the floor a few final licks before joining her.

Ben said, "I guess we'd better get dressed for dinner and slipped from the room with Maggie, George and Alistair at his heals. Jay stuck his head around the door. Surveying the carnage he said, "Damn! I should have snagged a few more of those cheese things while I had the chance."

"Oh shut up and help me clear away this mess. Here, slice this." I handed him a baguette. Fortunately, I had made a batch of Tapenade the day before and there were always olives, roasted peppers and marinated mushrooms. It wasn't a total disaster. "Where the hell is your brother?" I snapped.

"Hey! Don't yell at me. I didn't chuck the food on the floor. I told you. Lee and Alberto went to get a load of hay."

"That was hours ago. They should have been back by now. Which truck did they take?"

"The stake-bed I think."

"Ah hell, then they've probably broken down someplace. I don't know why your grandfather insists on keeping that old clunker."

"He says he keeps it because he doesn't have to have a PhD in computer sciences to work on it. Anyway, Lee and Alberto probably dropped off at Jack's Place for a beer after they loaded up. Who all's coming to this shindig tonight?"

"Father Sean of course, Charley, Ross, and Allen, and someone new, Lacey Coleman. She's the one opening the art gallery on the plaza."

"Lee know Allen's coming?"

"I think so."

"Then he probably won't show. He doesn't like Allen."

"I didn't know that. Why not?"

"Says he doesn't want a cop for a step father."

"That's ridiculous! Allen's not interested in me."

"Ah Ma! Wake up. He is too."

"No he's not, and don't call me Ma. It's Charley he's interested in."

"Charley may be interested in him, but Allen's interested in you Mom."

"Oh crazy. You really think so?"

"Ma's got a fellah...Ma's got a fellah..." he chanted with a huge grin.

"Stop that!" I snapped his butt with a tea towel. "And go get dressed. They'll all be here any minute and I need you and Ben to play host while I get things on the table."

"Grump's better at that. Sure wish I'd snagged a few more of those cheese things. That meat stuff looked good too." He slipped out of the room before I could take aim with my trusty tea towel again.

*　　*　　*

Dinner had gone well. Everyone had given the various Zinfandel experiments the thumbs up, but then they were close family and friends. One would hardly expect any of them to say, "Gee, Jo, this

12

really tastes like crap." Lacey had said she just wasn't used to so much garlic and onion. Ross, who's opinion I really trusted said she thought the Coq a Zin wasn't as rich as the Coq au Vin she had in Burgundy but then she supposed that most Americans would be totally repulsed by the traditional recipe. The chicken was always stewed in its own blood. I said I thought she was probably right and that I'd pass on that part of tradition. She suggested backing up the Zinfandel with just a touch of cream Sherry to smooth out the Zin and give the dish body and richness. I thought that was probably a good suggestion and decided to try it in a few days.

I was serving coffee and dessert in the living room in front of the fire. It was a pleasant autumn evening despite the fact that it had started raining, an early autumn rain. We didn't really need the fire but I find an empty fireplace depressing. The fire crackled comfortably. Maggie, George, Alistair, Marmalade and Fritz were in an intertwined pile in front of it, alternately snoozing and licking each others fur. Maggie was grooming Fritz, her huge tongue encompassing him with every swipe. Lee still hadn't shown up. I wasn't really worried, just a bit perplexed. He was an adult. He didn't live under my thumb, but this wasn't like him. He usually phoned when he was going to be late.

Charley was yet again trying to convince Ross to write her memoirs. "But Ross, you were there. You actually lived through it for Christ's sake. You not only lived through it, you were part of it!"

"Oh Charley, I appreciate your enthusiasm but I hardly think today's young people would have the slightest interest in the sentimental ramblings of an old woman."

"Sentimental ramblings hell Ross," I said. "You were commended by Churchill!"

"What about the time you cussed out de Gaulle on the phone?" said Allen.

"And captured a German spy. That's the story I like," added Jay. "I'm a young person and I'd love to read a book of your experiences during the war."

"Yes Ross. It's pretty hot stuff, to say nothing of the way you met your husband," said Father Sean. "You really should consider it.

Owning a bookstore should certainly put Charley in the know. She sees what sells every day."

"Well," Ross said taking a sip of her coffee. "I'll think about it. I suppose I'd have to buy one of those computer things first; and it's finding the time you know. I just have so much to do. It takes so much energy just to keep my old place from falling down, and despite having gone to an English public school,* I'm a terrible speller."

"That's what computers are for; and what makes you think you bloody English have a corner on good spelling?" Ben's part Irish ancestry bridled. The rest of us laughed.

"We have, or at least used to have, a corner on the spelling market because of the inhumane practices that was perpetrated against school children."

"What was so special about the English way?" Lacey asked.

"Ah well, when I was a girl, throughout the school day the school mistress would point to one of us with her pointer and call out a word. We had to stand, say the word, give its definition, spell it and use it in a sentence. If we got it wrong we had to go to the blackboard and write the word 100 times. When we had finished we had to turn, face the class and say, "God hates a lazy child. I was remiss. I shall do better."

"Why that's horrid," I said.

"Seems to me like our students could use a bit of that," Lacey said.

"Well, spelling is important of course, but that practice was quite humiliating. The same sort of thing was done with math. At the beginning of each day the teacher would call out a number, then she would say, multiply that by 27, now add 2,172, now subtract, 429, double that and divide by 14, or whatever set of numbers she was using that day. Then she would hand out paper on which we could only write our names and the final answer, which we had to work in our heads. This was considered just a little wake up exercise. Those of us who didn't have the correct answer had to stay in during the dinner hour and study. "

"I still say we could use a bit more formalized teaching methods here," Lacey insisted.

"Well Lacey dear," Ross said leaning forward a bit in her chair to reach the sugar bowl, "I'm proof that it didn't always work. In fact just the opposite. Anything mathematical makes me come sick and I'm a terrible speller, despite the fact that I love to read."

"Well, I think you're just making up excuses," Charley laughed. "You really should write that book. A computer or a secretary can take care of the spelling. Tell her Jo. You've said you're a rotten speller without your computer."

"But there's my garden, and the house, and..."

"Oh pooh," Charley countered.

"Hire a handy man. Hire a gardener," Allen said.

"But I enjoy gardening. I like to paint and patch..."

"Yes, but your stories are a part of history," Charley continued to urge. "You have a commitment to posterity."

"And just what's posterity ever done for me?" Ross said with a smile. "But, we'll see. Perhaps I might work on it some this winter. There isn't much to do in the garden in winter.

"You really were commended by Churchill?" asked Lacey registering total awe.

"Me and thousands of others."

"Come now Ross. Your commendation was special" Charley said. "Don't be over modest. It isn't becoming in someone your age. You have a right to be a bit smug about it.

If anyone's autobiographical ramblings would be of interest to the general public, Mrs. Rossini Beryl Collins-Bennett's would. This amazing lady, during her stint in the RAF in WWII, had been stationed on the south coast of England and had been a flight commander; quite an achievement for a woman at that time. While having an off-duty drink with friends at the local pub, she had apprehended a German spy and was commended by Churchill. She had dated one of the two men credited with the invention of the jet engine, and on one occasion had cussed out Charles de Gaulle over the phone. She had also owned and operated a successful chain of tea shops. She met an American Air Force Colonel near the end of the war, married him and moved to the U.S. In her late eighties, she was more active than many people I know half her age. I had always thought that she and Ben would have made a good match, but I suppose they were each too settled in their own lives or perhaps it was that she was thoroughly English and Ben, though born in California, was immitigably Irish, or part Irish. Yes, Ross's "sentimental ramblings," would make excellent reading.

"If we're talking about books," Ross said, "I think Jo's book about Zinfandel should be just the beginning. I think she should write a biography about Haraszthy and intersperse it with information about Zinfandel and her Zinfandel recipes."

"What is all this about Zinfandel?" Lacey asked. I've been hearing about Zinfandel ever since I came to Sonoma. Admittedly, I enjoy it but what is so special about it? It seems to have almost cult status around here. I had never heard of it until I moved here."

"Well, until recently it was mostly a California thing," I said. "It's thought that the grape originated right here in Sonoma at Haraszthy's Buena Vista Winery. Have you been there yet?"

"And who is this Haraszthy person I hear about?"

"You should ask Father Sean about that since he's a descendant."

"Oh?" Lacey turned to Father Sean, eager for a story.

As Sean obligingly began an abrogated history of the California wine industry and his family's part in it I got up and went to the window. It was raining harder now which only increased my concern about Lee. Allen got up too and came to stand by me. He put a hand on my shoulder. "I'm sure he's all right. I called in. There haven't been any accidents. He probably had car trouble. You said he was driving that old stake-bed of Ben's."

"I suppose you're right, but nonetheless..."

Just then, a pair of headlights glittered through the rain accompanied by the unmistakable chug and rattle of the old truck. A few minutes later, the back door slammed and I knew Lee was on the service porch taking off his boots. I gave a sigh of relief.

"I told you," Allen said with a warm smile.

"Anything left to eat," Lee called.

"Where the hell have you been with my truck?"

"Thanks Grump. Nice to see you too," Lee said as he filled a plate from the remains on the dining table.

When he walked into the living room I gasped. "What happened to you? Look at your face! Where have you been? How did that happen?"

"Whoa! One question at a time Ma. Hi everyone." He sat down on the raised hearth and started eating.

"Don't call me Ma."

"O.K. Ma." Everyone laughed.

"This is really good Mom," he said through a mouthful of chicken and pasta.

"Hey! Don't think you're too big to get smacked for talking with your mouth full." Everyone laughed again.

"O.K. Out with it Bro." Jay said. "So what the hell happened to your face?"

"Hey! What's with the third degree. The truck broke down. That's all."

"Six hours' worth?"

"We had a beer at Jack's Place after we got her started; met some people..."

"What happened to your face?" I asked. There were several deep scratches across one cheek.

"Got hit in the face with a branch while we were working on the truck. Come on. Let me eat. I'm starved."

So much for gracious after dinner conversation. Our guests, somewhat embarrassed, started an exodus, each thanking me and assuring me they would love to stay but had pressing business that required them to be up early the next day. Swell.

Before leaving however, Father Sean asked Lacey for her address and phone number. He said that since she was interested in Sonoma history he thought she would enjoy coming to his family's annual Zinfandel Harvest Festival.

Chapter 3

The smell of fresh muffins just out of the oven makes for a good start to the day. I try to keep muffins around when the guys are all working in the winery, besides. They make a wonderful air freshener, far better than anything in an aerosol can. This morning I had made what the boys called, Ma's Marvelous Munchable Muffins.

It had continued to rain most of the night and rain hard. This morning however, was a golden autumn day. Fortunately, most of the grapes had been gotten before the rain. Ben was out assessing if what remained on the vines was worth harvesting.

I would love to have been out in the vineyard or the winery with Ben and the boys, but no, I had this blasted book to finish and the deadline was fast upon me. I was puttzing about in the kitchen; cleaning up from last night, baking the muffins, anything to forestall the inevitable task of getting to my desk. I poured a second cup of coffee and stole a few more tranquil moments sitting on the back porch stoop. I loved the crush. Crate upon crate of grapes were stacked in the space between the big old barn and the winery. The heady aroma of fresh fruit filled the air and clouds of bees were busy trying to retrieve what they felt was their own. There was something magical about knowing that those truckloads of raw grapes would one day be bottles of fine wine. I sighed and turned back to the cluttered kitchen.

I had nearly finished with the kitchen when the phone rang.

"Hi Jo. Allen here. Wanted to thank you for last night. Everything was great, particularly the chicken. Great recipe. I'm sure your publisher will be pleased."

"Well, thanks. Yes, I think it's a keeper."

"Also, Jo...how about dinner sometime this week?"

"That'd be fine, but I'll have to let you know. I have to finish the book. Give me a call in a few days. I should know by then if there is any chance of my being able to make my deadline. O.K.?"

"Sure ... Ah ... by the way, when I got in this morning one of the boys told me there was a bit of a problem last night..."

I could tell he was apprehensive about continuing. "Oh?"

"Yeah ... Well ..., It seems Lee was in a bit of a fisticuffs with that kid Alberto who works for Ben."

"And..."

"And nothing much...There wasn't a report made. The officer was driving by Jack's Place and saw them tussling in the parking lot...thought he'd better stop and break it up. That little redhead, Ginger Sloan was with them."

"Oh crap. I thought Lee was through with her ages ago. So...what happened?"

"That's about it. The officer broke it up. Lee got in the truck. Alberto refused his offer to drive him home. The officer tried to give the girl a lift but she refused as well. I just thought you ought to know.

"Sure Allen...thanks."

"I'm sure it's nothing, Jo. I'll call you in a few days about dinner."

"Yeah...sure..." and I hung up.

"As I started back to work Lee came into the kitchen. "Hey Mom. Grump wants to know if the muffins you were making are ready yet."

"Good God!" I exclaimed when I looked at him. Last nights scratches were swollen and puffy and what had been a bit of redness around his eye had developed into a hum-dinger of a shiner. "You look like something the cat drug in. You didn't get that from a branch. I think we'd better have a talk, Lee. Sit down please. That was Allen on the phone. He said you and Alberto got into it last night in front of Jack's Place and that Ginger was involved."

"Ah hell, Mom. Alberto was being an asshole and Ginger's a tramp." He poured himself a cup of coffee and snagged a fresh muffin off the counter.

"So what changed your mind? You used to think she was pretty hot stuff."

"Too damn hot for me. Alberto can have her and welcome. I just hope he doesn't catch something."

"Are you in danger of having caught something?"

"Hell no Ma. No way. Not with her"

"Don't call me Ma! And how come not with her? You seemed pretty thick a few weeks ago. I didn't like it much, but I assumed you'd become intimate."

"Hey! This isn't the kind of conversation a guy wants to have with his mother over coffee and donuts."

"I don't do donuts. I do muffins."

"Whatever...anyway, I found out she's only sixteen and there's no way I'm going there."

"So, if you weren't going with her any more what were you and Alberto fighting about?"

He took a swallow of coffee, leaned back in the old kitchen chair and stuck his long legs out in front of him. "Well, so, we stopped into Jack's Place for a beer after we picked up the feed. And yes, Mom, the truck did break down and it took us a couple of hours to get it started."

"Hmm ..."

"Really Ma ..., uh, ... sorry, Mom. And so, we're sitting there at the bar having a beer and Ginger walks in. How she gets away with it I don't know. Everyone knows she's not twenty-one. Anyway, so she comes up to me and tries to climb into my lap while we're sitting there. She knocked over my beer and I shoved her off, so she starts making up to Alberto and he goes for it. Jesus, you should have seen it. She climbed into his lap and sat facing him with her arms around his neck and her legs wrapped around his waist; her dress up to her navel, and all she was wearing underneath was a pair of thong butt-floss panties, bright red. So anyway, she and Alberto are damn near making it right there on the bar stool. I said I had to leave and

20

asked Alberto if he was coming and I went outside. Alberto and Ginger followed me and Alberto said we were giving Ginger a ride home. I said no way, I didn't want her in the truck...well, one thing leads to another and we got into it. Ginger started screaming obscenities at me and scratched my face and then the cops came and I came home. Alberto must have got home somehow because he showed up for work this morning.

I was about to suggest that he have the doctor look at his face when the door slammed and Jay burst into the room. He was panting from running and took a moment to catch his breath before gasping, "Quick Mom! Call 911! Call the sheriff's department! Call Allen! There's a body in the grapes!"

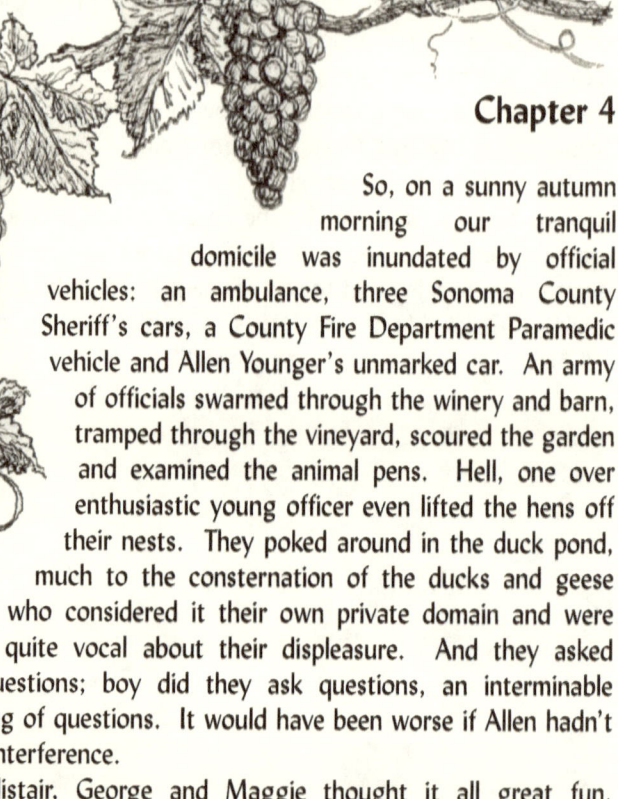

Chapter 4

So, on a sunny autumn morning our tranquil domicile was inundated by official vehicles: an ambulance, three Sonoma County Sheriff's cars, a County Fire Department Paramedic vehicle and Allen Younger's unmarked car. An army of officials swarmed through the winery and barn, tramped through the vineyard, scoured the garden and examined the animal pens. Hell, one over enthusiastic young officer even lifted the hens off their nests. They poked around in the duck pond, much to the consternation of the ducks and geese who considered it their own private domain and were quite vocal about their displeasure. And they asked questions; boy did they ask questions, an interminable string of questions. It would have been worse if Allen hadn't run interference.

Alistair, George and Maggie thought it all great fun, running, leaping, sniffing, yapping and baying. They loved company and to them this was just a big party, particularly after the press began showing up. More company! More excitement! What more could a dog want.

I was flummoxed that the press got wind of the situation so quickly. Jay told me that they must have a radio tuned to the police frequency, damn their hides. Allen, bless him, informed the members of the Fourth Estate that this was a crime scene where evidence was still being gathered and that their presence could jeopardize the gathering of that evidence. When they tried to spew doggerel about freedom of the press he politely but firmly explained that there was a great difference between freedom of the press and sensationalism and that the presence of unofficial persons could only compromise the gathering of evidence and that he was sure they didn't want to be charged with obstruction of justice. He said that the department would be calling a press meeting as soon as they had anything to disclose. Grudgingly, T.V. cameras were packed back into vans, cables rolled up and reporters left, but not before having tromped through the garden snapping irreverently and inappropriately at anything they deemed interesting; things like the underwear I had sun bleaching on the clothesline, the beer cans and an Irish whisky bottle waiting to be recycled and a bucket of wet garbage waiting to be carried out to the compost.

"Excuse me Lady," one photographer said, attempting to push past me and into the kitchen. "I just need to get a few shots of the inside of the house."

"Not unless you plan on loosing your balls," Ben shouted, purple with rage and near an apoplectic fit.

They all finally left; or at least withdrew to the bottom of the drive where they set up their equipment and got out their telephoto lenses. Damn but I do hate the press sometimes.

Ben grumbled about the mess that was being made in the winery. He followed behind the officers and forensic team fiercely glowering and muttering with every crate that was moved or cabinet that was opened. Allen tried mollifying him with explanations and promises that everything would be set to rights when they were finished, to which Ben only snorted. I really felt sorry for poor Allen. He was after all only trying to do his job and Ben's attitude wasn't helping.

Two of the forensic team grumbled about the number of tire tracks left in the mud by last night's guests and this morning's onslaught of press vehicles. I think it was their job to measure the tracks or take pictures of them or something. Two other men were pouring a plaster like substance into some of the tire tracks. Others were picking up bits and pieces of assorted stuff and putting it into baggies including some shards of red plastic found near a stack of crates. Jay said it looked like part of a tail light. As soon as they found it they inspected the tail lights of all of our vehicles but found them all intact.

Finally, after what seemed like hours, the sheriff's cars all left, followed by the ambulance with the body of Ginger Sloan. Allen gave my arm a squeeze and said he'd call. I knew it wasn't going to be about dinner.

We somberly went into the kitchen and I started a fresh pot of coffee. Ben went to the bar and poured himself a hefty draught of Tullamore Dew.

"So, what the hell happened?" I asked.

"We were just going along like usual," Jay said. "We'd dumped about six bins of grapes into the crusher. I had another crate on the fork lift and was just about to tilt it in when an arm plops out of it! I couldn't see it but Grump and Alberto started shouting and waving their arms so I stopped and climbed down to see what all the fuss was about and sure as hell, there was an arm dangling over the edge of the crate. Grump shut down the crusher and I lowered the crate back down and ran into the kitchen to tell you to phone. You know the rest. This really sucks; and I'm sorry Lee. I know you went out with her for a while."

"That's been over for quite a while, but it still sucks. She was pretty messed up but that's no reason to kill someone. Anyway ... how the hell did she wind up here, and in a box of grapes?"

"And in my old growth Zinfandel at that," Ben grumbled. "We'll have to chuck the whole batch now? Damn!" He downed the remains of his Tullamore Dew. "What the hell now," he spat when we heard another car coming up the drive.

"It's O.K.," Jay said, turning from the window. "It's just Father Sean."

"Oh good," I said. "I could certainly could use his company right now. We all could. Good morning Sean. Have a cup of coffee and sit down. We have quite a lot to tell you."

"Anything to do with the cavalcade of official vehicles I met on Arnold Road and that phalanx of press out there? I felt like a blockade runner when I turned up your drive. They snapped my picture and tried to stop the car and ask questions."

"Christ! Those damn vultures still out there?" Ben growled. "Coffee hell! He's going to need a belt of the Dew for this one. You

24

start filling him in. I'm going out to tell Alberto to go on home. I hardly think we'll be doing any more work today." He and his dogs left for the winery. I poured Father Sean a mug of coffee and Lee got him a double shot of the Tullamore and we began to relate the morning's happenings to him.

"That poor girl," Sean finally said. I know her family isn't of the Roman faith but I'll say a prayer for her. Quite a sad lot, her family."

"I don't know anything about her other than that Lee saw her for a while," I said.

"She was total trash," Jay spat. "Don't see what Lee ever saw in her."

"Thanks Bro. I appreciate you as well. And I didn't exactly see her. She saw me. Just sort of showed up wherever I was; hung around, hung on me, tried to make it look like we were a number."

"See what I mean? She was just a piece of easy trash."

"Jay," Father Sean put in. "Under the circumstances I think you might speak a little kinder."

"Yah. Sure Father. I'm sorry. No matter what she was she didn't deserve having her brains bashed in."

"Often," Father Sean continued, "people find it difficult to rise above their circumstances. She and the rest of her family live in a grubby little single-wide mobile home in a very trashy trailer park in Agua Caliente. It's not the most idyllic circumstances for a young lady to be growing up in. The father never seems to be able to keep a job because he's drunk most of the time. There's also a boy about twelve and a younger boy and girl.

"No mother?" I asked.

"No, the mother just up and left about a year ago. It's quite a sad situation. Like I said, I don't think they're Catholic but they come to us for assistance; the food bank, clothing, etc."

"Jeez," Jay said. "I didn't know any of that."

"Yes," Father Sean continued, "and she in, ... was, just about the only mothering the younger kids got. The father doesn't seem to give a real damn. Sometimes he's off for days at a time, leaving Ginger to care for them all. I've been trying to get the authorities to step in and do something but it's so hard. Social services are understaffed, under-funded and over-worked."

"That's terrible," I said. "I had no idea ..."

"Neither did I," Lee said. "She told me her dad was a service rep of some sort and that they lived in Glenn Ellen. She told me her mother died of cancer and that her father was so heartsick that he never dated or saw other women."

"Wishful thinking," Father Sean said. "She didn't like her own world so she made one up. Well, people; I am so sorry for what has happened. I must be on my way. I have several appointments. I'll say a prayer for the poor girl at Vespers, I'll pray for you all."

"Thank you Sean," I said. He embraced each of us before leaving.

Chapter 5

The remains of the day were tedious. The phone began to ring. The press and media kept pressing for interviews, to which I was curt and Ben was out and out rude, telling them to ... well, you can imagine.

I made a pile of sandwiches and left them on the kitchen table for lunch, then tried to get back to work on my book, but to no avail, so I turned on the T.V. to catch the noon news. I should have known better. Yep, there we were, splattered all over the screen in a chaos of cop cars, sheriffs men, barking dogs, (there were lots of shots of Alistair, George and Maggie,) and the underwear, recycling and garbage. I was mortified. It made our lovely home look like something out of "The Grapes of Wrath." I hadn't realized before just how damning the media expression "declined to make a statement at this time," or "refused to talk to reporters" could be.

The anchor, talking over a prolonged shot of the clothesline said, "... and our reporters were turned away from the Penella home, where the body of a young woman was found early this morning in a box of grapes, by family friend, Sonoma County Sheriff's Department detective, Allen Younger..." 'Bin you ass hole," I muttered under my breath, "a bin of grapes.' "...of It is not yet known if the girl had been sexually assaulted or not. The two Penella boys one of who had been dating the girl, refused to speak to our reporters..." the screen switched from the clothesline and my underwear to the shot of the recycling with the beer bottles and Ben's empty Irish whiskey bottle. " ... And now we go to location where Dave Crofter is waiting with an on the spot update."

"Yes Joan, as you can see we are here outside the Penella place. We were ordered off the property this morning and the members of the Penella family are still refusing to talk with us. One of our cameramen was threatened by the cantankerous patriarch of the clan, Ben Penella. We have been told that old man Penella is well armed and not above using his arsenal to protect his own. There is also a pack of large dogs that patrols the property... Back to you Joan."

"Thank you Dave. More on this breaking story; we have just learned that there was an incident outside Jack's Place last night involving, the murdered girl, Penella and Hispanic agricultural worker Alberto Mendez who is employed by Ben Penella. Mendez had also been dating the murdered girl. We will keep you informed as we get more information on this breaking story ... now to you Dick for the weather..." I was shocked, stunned, mortified ... Ben was apoplectic with rage and the boys were dumbstruck.

Almost immediately following the noon news the phone began ringing itself off the wall until I unplugged it. Ben and the boys went to the winery to begin cleaning up after the morning's barrage of official persons, each of whom seemed to find it necessary to look behind and in every barrel, crate, case, box and piece of equipment. Ben grumbled bitterly as he instructed Jay to use the forklift and carry the contaminated grapes out between the vines, dump them, and spread them for mulch. They finally came back into the kitchen as it was nearing dark.

"What do you guys want for dinner?" I asked as they trudged in.

"Oh, potato something-or-other," said Ben listlessly.

"Rice I guess," said Jay.

"Pasta'd be O.K," Lee said.

My guys were definitely into carbs, even if today their enthusiasm left something to be desired. "Pasta sounds good," I said. "There's lots of basil and tomatoes in the garden that need using." I picked up my basket and went into the garden. My table garden had the ability to elevate my mood no matter how low it had sunk. I started with the tomatoes; Romas for the pasta and some heirlooms for the salad. Then I gathered a variety of salad greens and some green onions and finally a large bouquet of fresh Basil. I thought I'd make some fresh gnocchi in a tomato and basil sauce, with roasted garlic. I knew both boys loved it and although Ben's half-Celtic roots displayed themselves in his love of potatoes, his Italian ancestry was not to be pushed aside. Ben also loved pasta.

Cloves of garlic were gently roasting in a cast iron skillet and I had just started to wash the greens and herbs when the phone rang. "Hello? Mrs. Mendez? What? Please, Mrs. Mendez. Slow down. I can't understand you. What? What? Oh no! Calm down Mrs. Mendez. Calm down. Ben will be right over." I hung up the phone.

"Ben, you have to go right over to Mrs. Mendez. The sheriff just came and arrested Alberto and his mother is hysterical and doesn't know what to do."

"Ah Christ." Ben spat. "Call Father Sean and have him meet us there. My Spanish isn't good enough for a situation like this." He went to the service porch and pulled on his boots. "You'd better come too. This sounds like a woman's touch might be needed."

"Sure," I said. "You guys'll have to fend for yourselves for supper. Make a salad. There's chicken and meatloaf in the fridge, and you can..."

"Mom...Don't worry. We aren't exactly helpless in the kitchen you know," Jay said. "You were planning gnocchi so ... we'll make gnocchi. Don't worry. We'll leave some for you and Grump; and yah, we'll clean up."

"Thanks guys. You're terrific. I'm coming," I called to Ben as I scooped up a coffee cake I had made earlier, put it in a box and brought it with me. Crumb topped coffee cake is a great solace in time of crisis.

The Mendez home was a modest clapboard house built sometime in the 1930's. It was tucked into a vineyard on the outskirts of Sonoma. Mrs. Mendez had turned the quarter acre around it into a lush garden which kept her family amply supplied with fresh vegetables and provided her with the flowers she weekly took to her church. A large fig tree at the back of the house provided shade and fruit. To one side there was a tee-pee made from long poles up which climbed Scarlet Runner beans. This was a favorite playground for Alberto's three small sibling. Bougainvillea almost obscured the front of the house while hollyhocks and sunflowers, taller than their mistress flanked the doorway. When we arrived Mrs. Mendez was standing on the porch wringing her hands with her three small children clinging to her skirts.

Alberto was the major source of support for his mother and siblings. Mrs. Mendez supplemented their income by selling her excellent fresh hand-made tamales. Sure, it's against the law to sell a home-made food product door-to-door without a certified kitchen and food handler's license but no one gave a damn. They were good tamales.

"Oh, Mr. Ben," she wailed. They take my Alberto away. He's a good boy. He do nothing wrong. He works hard. He's not a bad boy. Why they take my Alberto. He no be able to come to work if he in jail. What we going to do Mr. Ben? My Alberto; he's a good boy."

We went into her warm, fragrant kitchen. Fragrant with coffee, vanilla, cinnamon, bundles of herbs, and ristras; the long ropes of dried chilies that hang in most Latino kitchens. One might think that bringing a coffee cake into such a kitchen was like bringing coals to Newcastle, but a gesture of hospitality can never be out of place. I set the coffee cake on the table and she began pouring out cups of strong cinnamon and vanilla-flavored coffee. Just then Father Sean drove up.

As he came into the kitchen she cried, "Oh Father O'Malley...My Alberto's a good boy. He no kill that naughty gorl." Then she lapsed into Spanish, "El es un católico bueno. El va a la iglesia cada día. El trabaja duramente. El no podría matar nadie," and she began to cry.

"There, there my daughter," he said taking her hands. "I know Alberto's a good boy. Of course, he didn't kill that girl. We'll get to the bottom of this. Have faith, daughter, have faith."

She again launched into a rapid fire dialogue in Spanish interrupted frequently with sobs and tears and wringing of hands. The youngest of her brood climbed into my lap and peeked into the box with the coffee cake. She looked up at me with huge soft brown eyes and smiled. I smiled back and nodded my head in consent. She slipped her hand inside the box and began pinching off small bits of the crumb topping and popping them into her mouth. Then she smiled up at me again, leaned her head against my bosom and proceeded to fall asleep; quite an achievement I thought, given the commotion in the room.

Father Sean and Mrs. Mendez talked for a long while. Finally Father Sean got up, took both her hands in his, kissed them, placed them in her lap and kissed her on the forehead. I stood as well and handed her the sleeping child. "I'll follow you back to your place," he said as we left the kitchen and were getting into our cars.

When we got back to the house my guys were just finishing their supper. Yes, there was some left for us and no, they hadn't cleaned up yet. The kitchen looked like there had been an explosion at Williams-Sonoma. My marble baking slab was covered with flour and goo, there was flower on the floor and the stove was wearing a patina of olive oil, chopped onions, garlic and herbs. I looked in one of the pots. What on earth is this?" I asked.

"Your gnocchi recipe. We made it just the way you always do." Lee said. "Well, almost anyway. I thought it might be good with some blue cheese in the sauce."

"We don't have any blue cheese."

"Yes we did Ma. Way in the back of the fridge; a little piece. I crumbled that up and put it in."

"You didn't use up my precious little bit of imported Stilton," I gasped.

"If it was the little bit of blue cheese wrapped in gold foil in the back of the fridge, I guess we did."

"That was real imported Stilton. Eighteen dollars a pound plus shipping and you crumbled it into pasta!"

"It's really good Ma...Mom, try some."

I had to admit that it was quite nice but at eighteen dollars a pound I didn't predict I'd be crumbling Stilton into my gnocchi very often.

"So, what gives? Lee asked once we were all settled around the kitchen table.

"Yah," Lee asked, "What gives?"

"Well... the sheriffs came to the house to question Alberto because the girl's father raised a stink. After the little tussle you and Alberto had outside Jack's Place, Alberto walked the girl home."

"All the way to Agua Caliente? That's some walk, Jay said.

"Apparently they didn't have to walk all the way. Someone gave them a lift. Now all this is what Mrs. Mendez said Alberto told her. They got a lift to Ginger's home. When they got there the girls father came storming out brandishing a shotgun and screaming and yelling about a filthy spick messing around with his little girl. He was violent and very drunk. He smacked the girl and sent her into the house. Alberto got back into the car and they drove off.

"Then today, the father kept ranting and raving that Alberto had killed his little girl. Said he had come back for her after the father had gone to bed because he had got up in the middle of the night and she was gone. The sheriffs did go to Alberto's to question him since it appeared that he was the last person to see her alive. They searched the house and found Alberto's old twenty-two and hauled him in."

"Hell! Ben spat. "That wasn't Alberto's twenty-two. It was mine. I loaned it to Mrs. Mendez to shoot the rabbits that get into her garden. Damn it!"

"O.K." Lee said, "So what was he arrested for, murder? That's ridicules. She had her head bashed in, not shot."

"I'm not really sure. Mrs. Mendez was so upset it was hard to get the story straight."

"I'll have to go down and see what this is all about," Ben said, "and get my twenty-two back!"

"I'll go with you," Father Sean said.

They were gone for what seemed like hours, but when they returned Alberto was with them. Ben had stood bail. I put on a fresh pot of coffee.

"So what's up? "Jay blurted. "What did they charge you with? They're not trying to say you killed Ginger are they? That's pretty stupid. She wasn't shot. She had her brains bashed in." Leave it to my youngest to be subtle and tactful.

"I'm not quite sure. I don't really know what happened." Alberto hung his head and stared at his laced fingers resting on the table in front of him. His mouth was pressed into a tight line.

Father Sean spoke. "Alberto's embarrassed to tell you, but two years ago he was convicted of possession of marijuana. He's still on probation and not allowed to have firearms, so when they found the twenty-two they brought him in on violation of probation. He goes back to court next week. We'll know more then."

We talked with his attorney from the public defender's office this evening and explained about the gun," Ben said. "Hell, Alberto didn't even know it was in the house. His mother had put it up on a high shelf so the kids wouldn't get it."

"Evidently they went to the house to question him since the girl's father made such a stink and said Alberto was the last one to see her alive."

"I don't understand," Alberto said. "Why me? I hardly knew her. Just met her last night. I had seen her around. Kerumba! Everyone had, but I didn't know her. Besides, Rod was there too."

"Because the cops are a bunch of racist, right wing Fascist bastards!" Ben spat.

"Do shut up Ben. This is no time to get on your political high horse," I said with some irritation. I consider myself pretty far to the left of center politically; however, sometimes Ben's over the top attitude could be inappropriate and downright annoying.

"Rod? Rod who?" asked Jay.

"Rod Gardino. He's the one who came along and gave us a ride. And hell. I wasn't even with Ginger then. When we got in the car she pushed into the front seat and I sat in back. And she was all over Rod. He had to keep shoving her off him so he could drive. It was embarrassing, you know? And she said she had to see him again."

Chapter 6

Alberto didn't go to court until the following Tuesday. His attorney from the public defender's office explained what he'd been told by Ben about the gun. She also pleaded that he was the major support of his mother and younger siblings, and she brought up the fact that Alberto was not the only one to have seen Ginger that night; that Alberto and Rod Gardino had driven her home together in Rod's car.

The D.A., however, embarrassed by the girl's very vocal father, so vocal in fact that the judge had him removed from the court room, made a rather half hearted case against Alberto. The end result was that Alberto was allowed to go home; his probation was extended for another year (which seemed unfair but better than other possibilities) and was warned not to leave the area because he might be needed for questioning again.

*   *   *

"Jesus Mom," Jay said over coffee and fresh pumpkin spice muffins, his favorite, the next morning. "What the hell would have happened if they'd kept Alberto in jail? Mrs. Mendez and the kids really need Alberto at home. They couldn't survive without him. And he's such a good worker." He reached for his third muffin. "Grump couldn't get along without him here either. Sure, Lee and I love working in the winery but face it. As soon as classes start each year we aren't around enough to be of much help, what with homework and practice. And Alberto is a real help, not like a lot of guys who don't know what the hell to do without it being more work to show them than for Grump to just do it himself. Alberto's a really bright guy. He ought to be in college too. It's totally dumb that he was ever arrested in the first place." He was buttering yet another muffin. "Hey, these other muffins are really good too, not as god as the pumpkin, but really good... funny looking though," he said through a mouthful. "How come they're purple?"

"They have grapes and wine in them; Zinfandel."

"Zinfandel, of course, the book. Well I'm not sure the color is all that appealing but they sure taste good. I still think the pumpkin ones are my favorite."

"Thanks."

"He ought to sue the county for harassment and malicious mischief," Ben grumbled as he gave the morning paper a good shake.

"What?" I asked.

"Alberto! He ought to sue the county. They're only harassing him because he's a poor Mexican farm laborer. Why the very foundation of this nation is dependent on the sweat of people like Alberto!" He slammed his fist down on the table and his coffee cup jumped.

"Oh for Christ Sake Ben," I said, then, "Now who the hell's that."

The dogs, our early warning system, announced a car coming up the drive. It was Alberto's old pickup. His mother was with him. She was carrying a big basket which proved to be filled with her delectable homemade tamales. "For you Mister Ben," she beamed. "For you...for helping my boy, Gracias, gracias Señor Ben, para ayudar mi Alberto," and she flew into a torrent of tearful Spanish. Then she threw her arms around me, almost smothering me in her grateful embrace. I didn't feel I'd been of any aid at all, but evidently she did.

Alberto too, was expressing his gratitude to Ben when the dogs announced the arrival of yet another vehicle. This time it was Allen Younger. He gave a perfunctorily knock at the screen door on the service porch and came in. I poured him a cup of coffee. Mrs.

Mendez gave him a cold stare, then said, "Alberto! We go now," and she swept from the room. I watched them climb into the battered old pickup and rattle down the drive with Alistair, George and Maggie providing a joyful though raucous escort. I watched her go with a lightness of heart I hadn't felt since the poor girls body was discovered. Turning back and looking at Allen sitting at the kitchen table however, my spirits sank again. "Allen? What's wrong? You look like the grim reaper."

He slumped down in his chair, sighed and took a sip of coffee. "Ben. You can come pick up your twenty-two," he said. Everything checks out and all new charges have been dropped. Alberto's still, of course, on probation for the old drug charge."

Ben let out a snort of contempt. "Wouldn't be if he was the son of a rich white man."

"Don't evade the issue," I said. "Out with it. What's up?"

"Jo, I'm afraid I have to ask Lee to come down with me for questioning."

"What the fuck for?" Ben spat.

"What? Oh Allen." I sank into a chair opposite him. "If you're joking it's damn well not funny!"

"This is no joke, Jo. Too many people saw the fight between Lee and Alberto and they saw Lee and Ginger get into it as well. I need to take him in with me for questioning. It's just routine."

"Being taken in by the local gendarme is far from routine," I said.

I'm sure nothing will come of it. I came because I thought it would be better than having a pair of uniforms turn up on your door step."

"You're damn right nothing'll come of it!" Ben raged, jumping from his chair. "You bloody damn power-hungry Nazi! I'll sue! I'll sue the department. I'll sue the county. I'll sue you too God damn it! Give someone a little authority..."

"Oh for Christ-sake, shut up Ben," I snapped. "Allen'll get things straightened out. We know Lee didn't do anything. It'll be O.K." Despite my brave words, my heart was thumping so hard it felt like it would jump right through my shirt.

"That's right. Just a few questions," Allen reiterated.

"What questions?" Jay had just returned to the kitchen.

"Allen is going to take Lee in for questioning about that girl."

"The hell you are! No way! Lee hasn't done anything! Grump! We can't let him do this."

"Don't get excited. He's just going to be asked a few questions."

"Questions my ass!" Ben exploded. "You can take your questions and get the hell off my property!"

"Now Ben," Allen tried to sooth and he placed a hand on Ben's arm. Ben knocked it off vehemently and glowered into the younger man's face.

"That's O.K. Grump," Lee said. "There's no problem. I'll go with Allen, answer a few questions and be right back. Can we have chicken for dinner Ma?"

"Sure, if you don't call me Ma," I said as lightly as I could.

"Things'll be fine Bro," Jay said, giving his brother a friendly thump on his shoulder. "This'll teach you to keep your pants zipped."

"Not without my attorney there you won't answer any questions," Ben started up again. This is just another right wing plot. That dead girl is just an excuse. You're being targeted because of my political activities. It's just a crude attempt of the establishment to muffle the voice of the people." He stood with his clenched fist in the air like some biblical prophet, although my image of a biblical prophet had always been of a tall lean man in flowing garments and with a sweeping white beard, not an irate Santa in Levis. "They'll stop at nothing to smash the rebellion."

Sometime I'll have to sit down with Ben and explain that the peoples rebellion of the 60's has been over for quite some time and that shocking though he might find it, he wasn't much of a thorn in the establishment's side. It is highly unlikely that the FBI or the CIA had Ben Penella on their "most dangerous" list.

"This is stooping pretty low," he continued. "If you want me, take me," and he thrust his arms out to be cuffed, "Don't try to get to me through my innocent grandson."

"Oh can it, Ben," I said with considerable irritation

"This hasn't anything to do with you," Allen said, trying to hide a

smile, "not unless you were trying to make time with the girl too."
He made the mistake of chuckling.

"What...you think I couldn't...pretentious young pup...let me tell
you...I could still..."

"Grump! Let it go! You're going to make things worse," Lee
said.

"And you can bet your bottom dollar things'll continue to get
worse as long as these right wing, reactionary, Fascist, money-
grubbing oil barons are in control of things." He punctuated his
statement by trying to punch his own hole in the Ozone layer above
his head with his forefinger.

Despite the seriousness of the situation we were all having a hard
time not laughing. Ben continued to harangue poor Allen as he and
Lee headed to the car, and of course because of the excitement,
Alistair, George and Maggie had leapt into action, which did little to
add solemnity to the situation, particularly when Maggie climbed into
the car and began clawing at the glove compartment where she knew
Allen kept his dog treats.

"You should probably have your family attorney meet us at the
station," Allen said as he got into his car.

My heart sank as I watched my oldest son ride down the drive in
Allen's unmarked car. Ben continued with his tirade on the right
wing activities of the establishment. "Oh shut up," I shouted, "and
go call Jason."

Chapter 7

Living as we did, surrounded by acres of vineyards and orchards, you might think we'd be spared the intrusions of curiosity seekers, but no; thanks to the dubious joys of technology, the phone began ringing itself off the wall about thirty minutes after I watched Lee disappear down our drive. The first was Sylvia Adams.

"Oh my poor darling." Her condescending voice dripped Saccharin into the phone. "I know how frightfully difficult it must be to raise boys. I count myself so fortunate to have been blessed with two lovely girls. I know how dreadfully difficult this all must be for you."

"What the hell are you talking about?"

"Oh, now dear. You don't have to be brave with me. I know just what you are going through and how terribly, terribly difficult this must be for you."

Frightfully difficult. Dreadfully difficult. Terribly, terribly difficult. Sylvia never had been known for her scintillating conversation. "Sylvia, please. What are you going on about?"

"Oh, my poor brave dear. Why Jay, of course. Being arrested. And right after the shock of finding that poor dismembered girl floating in a barrel of wine..."

"Jesus," I thought, holding the phone out at arms' length for a moment, "just what I didn't need." Then into the phone, "Sylvia, it wasn't Jay, it was Lee. He has not been arrested. They just want to ask him a few questions. The girl wasn't dismembered and she wasn't floating in a wine barrel. She was found in a box of grapes.

"Well, ... that's what I was told by Ellen Chatterby and she said she heard it from the wife of a reporter who was on the scene."

"Well then, I guess there's nothing much else I can add since you obtained your information from such an authoritative source." Swell! Sylvia was the last person I wanted to talk to right now. Why Charley kept her on at the bookstore I had no idea. She didn't read, she didn't know anything about books and she didn't have a particularly winning way; and, she took an insidious joy in spreading unsavory gossip, sometimes to a detrimental degree.

"Don't worry darling. We're not busy at the moment. I'll lock up the store and be right over. I know you don't want to be alone at a time like this and I know it's what Charley would do if she were here. She's out of town for the day at a book show. You hang on darling. I'll be right there. We'll have a glass of wine and a ..."

"Sylvia. Don't come. I'm not alone. I'm in the very good company of my other son, my father-in-law, a large horse, three dogs, two cats, a dozen sheep and goats and about a million friendly honey bees."

"Oh how like you, to joke at a time like this. That just shows what a brave girl you are. But you don't have to be brave with me. We're too good of friends for that." I hardly knew her, and I didn't like her. "You hang on now. I'm locking up as we speak and I'll be there in just a few minutes, Darling."

"Sylvia, I am not alone and I don't want company." Or at least not yours, I muttered under my breath and hung up.

There were three more such calls in rapid succession. A while later Ross called. Her company I really would find comforting. "I'll be right over," she said. "Put the kettle on." At 80-something, not only did Rossini Beryl Collin-Bennett still drive, she drove a vintage Morgan, usually far too fast. She was in my kitchen in what seemed like minutes.

Shortly after Ross arrived and we were sitting in the kitchen with our tea, a strange car came up the drive.

"Shit!" Now what?" I got up and went to the back door. Two men climbed out. One had a large camera and began snapping away.

"Ms. St. John. Jack Grover. The National Exposé. A few words please. When was your son apprehended? Did he resist arrest? How do you feel about having a son who committed murder? I understand one of your employees beat the girl up in a bar before your son killed her. Were they working together? Jack," he called over his shoulder, "here, get a few shots of the mother, then take some where the body was found." He turned back to me. "We'd also like to get a few of your son's room. You know...sort of background stuff."

"Please," I said, bewildered by the barrage of questions. "What are you doing?"

"How long had your son been having an affair with the murdered girl? Did he kill her because she was pregnant?"

"What? ... I..."

Just then, the screen door slammed. "You drag your sorry asses off my property before I shoot em off!" Ben stood on the top step with an immense old firearm (one of many in his collection) leveled at the intruders.

"Ben!" I shouted aghast. "Put that down."

"Not 'till I see the backsides of these bastards heading down the drive. Sick-um," he hissed at the yelping tangle of fur leaping and frolicking around his legs. "Sick-um! Go on! Chew the bastards up! Get the hell out of here before I let my dogs tear you limb from limb!"

Alistair, George and Maggie of course, thought this was all great fun and continued to yelp and circle around Bens legs. The photographer made the mistake of choosing that moment to shoot off a flash. This instantly drew the dogs' attention. They careened down the steps in a furry mass, the largest and furriest leading the way, her huge red tongue lolling from her grinning mouth. Her front paws landed full force on the photographers' chest. The photographer went one direction, his camera in the other. Oh, what a wonderful game! How thoughtful of us to organize it for them.

Maggie stood on the prone photographer's chest, panting joyfully and dripping ropes of adhesive salvia onto his face. George assumed that it was a ball game and that the camera was the ball. He retrieved it in a single bound and headed across the drive and down towards the duck pond with it, before stopping to see if anyone else was joining in the fun.   Little Alistair, in the meantime, ran in frantic circles obviously trying to capture his own tail. Finally George decided that since no one was giving chase, perhaps it wasn't a ball game after all, so he settled down with the camera between his muddy paws and proceeded to gnaw on it until the back popped open allowing him to pull out the film and managed to wrap it around himself.

I remember thinking how much less entertaining this would have been had the camera been digital.   Needless to say, these members of the press did not continue with their interview. Mud covered and quaking, the photographer climbed into the car, clutching the remains of his camera to his chest. His companion hastily followed his lead, shouting platitudes about the freedom of the press over his shoulder. They drove off with Alistair, George and Maggie in hot pursuit. Little did they know that the dogs only wanted to play and that Ben's blunder-buss wasn't even loaded. Non-the-less I winced when I thought of what tomorrow's tabloid headlines would be.

No sooner had we all returned to the kitchen than another car came up the drive. This time it was Jason Alexander, our family attorney.

"So, how'd it go?" I asked trying to keep my voice light and unconcerned despite my racing pulse and pounding heart. "Where's Lee?" I asked, as I peered over his shoulder.

"You'd better sit down, Jo. It didn't go all that well."

"What do you mean? All they wanted to do was ask him a few questions. Where is he?"

"Yah! Where the hell's my grandson? What have those bastards done with him?"

"Keep your shirt on, Ben. Jo, sit down please. Hello Mrs. Collin-Bennett," he said with a nod to Ross.

"What gives?" asked Jay.

"Well..., they're holding Lee."

"What the hell d'ya mean they're holding him?" Ben snapped as he propped his blunderbuss in the corner.

"Good God, Ben! You haven't been brandishing that damn thing around have you?"

"Never mind about me! What's happened to my grandson? Why didn't you bring him home? Whad'ya think you get paid for?"

Jason turned from Ben to me. Jo, I really think you should sit down."

I sank into a kitchen chair, my heart pounding even harder and my hands clenched together so tightly the knuckles were white.

When the lab report came back there was skin tissue under the girl's nails. That, plus the scratches on Lee's face, was adequate probable cause. They took a tissue sample from Lee and they are keeping him until the results come back from the lab."

"Oh my God!" My hand automatically flew to my throat. "But I don't understand. Lee admitted that Ginger had scratched him."

There's more. She was pregnant. Do you have any idea just how deeply involved Lee was with her?"

"My brother wouldn't screw that piece of trash on a bet," Jay spat.

"I can't see why he dated her in the first place," Ben grumbled. "He could get any girl he wanted."

"He didn't date her," Jay sprang to his brother's defense. "She just sort of showed up and attached herself to him. Hell! She attached herself to anyone who'd let her. Lately she's been going after Rod Gardino. I think it's his car and wallet she likes."

"Rod? I thought he was engaged to that Stafford girl. Dianne, isn't it?" Ben asked.

"Yah, well, I guess he figures a little on the side won't hurt."

"Please!" I shouted. "This is totally irrelevant! I don't give a dam about who Ginger Slone is, ... was sleeping with. My son is in jail; accused of a horrible crime. Let's keep focused. Jason ...?"

"You're perfectly right dear," Ross said. "Here, let me pour you another cup-a." I have always been staggered that to the English, there is no problem so great that "... a nice hot cup-a ..." won't fix it right up.

"Please remember Jo, he hasn't been charged yet. They're just holding him pending the results of the lab test. He admitted she scratched his face; and of course, they're also waiting for the DNA results as to who the father of the baby may be."

Ben slammed his fist down so hard on the table that Ross's tea cup jumped. "God damn it all to hell, Jason. How the hell did you let it get this far? You should have done something. Why did you let them keep him in jail? I think you're getting too old to practice."

"Damn it Ben. I've a good mind to drop you as a client. My doctor said I was to eliminate stress in my life if I was to keep from having another heart attack, and over the past thirty years, you are probably responsible for half of it. Moreover, I'm not a criminal lawyer. I'm a paper pusher. I handle your tax problems; go over your contracts, rewrite your will every time you decide to change it leaving some pittance to this or that radical political organization. I only went with Lee today as a favor. You are most likely going to have to hire a really good criminal defense attorney."

"At least you could have gotten him out on bail."

"Bail hasn't been set yet, Ben. I tried. Bail won't be set until the results of the tests are back from the lab and he goes before the judge."

"Yah, and how long is that going to take?" Jay asked.

"How come Alberto got out?" I asked.

"Well, because..."

"Because he doesn't have a history of left wing political activities," Ben shouted. "That girl's death has nothing to do with it. The establishment will do anything to smear me and my family. Why, they've been after us since the 'Epic Campaign' in the '30's when my father..."

"Oh do shut up," I sighed.

"Ben, I hate to be the one to tell you this, but you aren't important enough for the establishment, as you call it, to have been after you for decades, so just wrap it up. We have more important matters to discuss. Here Jo. This is the card of a really excellent criminal attorney I work with sometimes. You might want to give her a call. I have to be in court in half an hour. I'll see what I can find out while I'm in town and give you a call. I know it's a foolish thing to say, but try not to worry too much. So far everything is just circumstantial. Chin up Jo." He gave me a kiss on the cheek. "And

44

listen to me Ben. I'm too God damn old to put up
with your tantrums and you're too damn old to have them. They
shook hands and he gave Jay a thump on the shoulder. Alistair,
George and Maggie escorted him to his car.

Chapter 8

I thought I should feel worse than I did. I thought I should be hysterical, or distraught; crying or screaming ... something ... What I felt was nothing... nothing at all. I just felt empty, I wanted something, and I didn't know what. Yes I did. I wanted a cigarette. I had quit smoking when I moved here. Ben was adamant about cigarettes. He didn't allow smoking in the house, in the barns or winery, near the animals, in the orchard or vineyards; in other words, no smoking on Ben's domain. Well, that's not precisely true. On long hot summer evenings when Ben was entertaining his cronies on the front veranda, they did smoke pipes and cigars and after Thanksgiving, Christmas and Easter dinner again, cigars and brandy were usually enjoyed. Despite his years, I found his adherence to the antiquated brandy and cigars ritual rather strange in one of Ben's avant-garde views. But then Ben was nothing if he wasn't an amazing collection of contradictions and surprises. All this aside, damn, I wanted a cigarette.

Despite events, life went on. Dust still settles, clothes still get dirty and bellies still empty. Grapes still ripen and need to be picked; and, publishers' deadlines still have to be met. Ben, Jay and Alberto spent most of their time working in the barns and winery and of course, despite the previous week's rain, the last of the grapes had to be brought in. There were goats to milk, weeds to pull, tomatoes to can, herbs to dry, meals to prepare, laundry to be done and that damn book to finish. My heart was in none of it; so, to hell with damn weeds, goats, grapes, tomatoes, and to hell with the damn book.

A cigarette was what I needed, no, wanted, and some time away from it all so I climbed into Betsey, my old V.W. bug and of course she wouldn't start. Frustrated, I lifted the hood and giggled the battery cables. This is a frequent ritual. Going anywhere in Betsey isn't a given. It's usually a labor vs. management negotiation. Management usually wins and I have learned that I am not management. Why I keep her I don't know. I've been promising myself I would replace the old jalopy with the advance from my next book for about six books but, something more pressing usually came up.

On the edge of town I stopped at a convenience store to pick up a pack of smokes and then headed for my favorite little cafe just off The Plaza in down town Sonoma. Amazingly, there was a parking space in front, which was a sort of miracle. There is never a parking place on Spain Street. As usual, the downstairs was packed out with tourists but I was relieved to find that the upstairs veranda was relatively empty. Just a couple at the far end and oh joy of joys, Father Sean and Ross sitting at a table overlooking the street below. I joined them, opened my pack of illicit smokes, lit up, inhaled deeply, reached for Father Sean's beer, and took a long drink. He hailed the waiter who had just come up to the veranda.

"We'll each have another and what are you having Jo? It's good to see you. What brings you to town?"

"I'll have the Heffevisen please, and an order of deep fried calamari. I just had to get out for a while."

"My poor love. I can't even begin to imagine what you must be going through," Ross said and patted my hand. "I won't even try. Just know that my heart goes out to you and anytime, day or night you need a friend I am here."

"You know that goes for me too Jo."

"Thank you both. It's good to know there are a few people who really care and aren't just morbidly curious gossip mongers. I could use a bit of good company right now. So, what brings you here in the middle of the afternoon?"

"Yes, well, I'm performing a wedding at the mission tomorrow and Ross came with me to give things a look. The parents of the bride are friends of hers and they have asked her to do the flowers."

"Yes," Ross said. "They don't want stiff formal arrangements, just big bouquets that look like they were picked from a garden and that's exactly what they're getting. I'll pick the flowers tomorrow morning and bring them to the chapel in the mission. I was going to call and ask if I could come pick some of your zinnias and sunflowers, and I wondered if Ben would mind if I took some grapevines as well. I think they make lovely arrangements this time of year when the leaves are just beginning to turn color."

"Of course, you may use any flowers I have, Ross, and with fifty acres of vines I'm sure Ben can spare a few grape leaves."

I looked over the railing as I tamped out my cigarette and reached for another. From this vantage point, you can look down on the mission across the street and do a bit of tourist watching, as our throng of visitors mill up and down the street and about the plaza. Despite Sonoma being such a high destination tourist attraction, it still somehow manages to retain a bit of a "home town" feel. Perhaps it's because our tourists are either interested in good wine or history. After all, a lot of California's history happened right here in the plaza. This is the sight of the 1846 "Bear Flag Rebellion." The Plaza also offers a walk through the history of California architecture. You will find everything from the adobe Mission founded in 1823, several classic Victorians, and the marvelously pink art deco Sebastiani Theatre, built in 1933.

"So, how are things going?" Father Sean asked after the waiter had set down our order.

I brought them up to date. "And as if things weren't bad enough," I continued, "this couldn't have happened at a worse time. We have to finish the harvest and the crush. I feel guilty as all hell having boogied out today and leaving the guys behind working their butts off, but I thought I just had to get away. I'm so glad to fine you two here. I truly need the diversion." I reached for another cigarette.

"Excuse me Ma'am," our young waiter said as he passed our table with a tray. "I'm afraid I'll have to ask you not to smoke. City ordinance about smoking in public you know."

"Oh, sorry. I forgot," and I snubbed it out. "Damn! I was really looking forward to smoking myself to death this afternoon."

"That's O.K." he said. "A lot of people forget." When he delivered the bottle of beer and a glass of white wine on his tray to the table at the end of the veranda, I noticed that the young man was Rod Gardino. He and the young lady did not appear to be too happy. He had raised his voice and we were able to overhear snatches of the conversation.

"Damn it Heather. I hope this isn't a sample of what life will be like after we're married? I won't live with suspicions and accusations."

"But Rod," and her voice broke, "I found a woman's shoe in your car."

"So, what's the big deal? What's all this fuss about a God damn shoe?"

"Well, it wasn't one of mine."

"So, big deal. So there was a shoe in the car...maybe I gave someone a ride..."

"And they just happened to leave one shoe in your car? Not likely."

"Well, maybe I took a load of old clothes to the thrift store. Maybe someone borrowed my car. I can't remember."

"Oh, Rod..." and she started to cry.

"God damn it Heather. I don't have to take this kind of crap." He stood up, threw some money on the table for the check and stomped away. The girl remained at the table, trying to control her emotions but it was easy to see she was on the verge of a good old-fashioned crying jag. As Rod passed our table, I couldn't help but notice that his face looked like he'd been mauled by a mountain lion.

"He's such an arrogant, little spoiled brat," said Ross. "I can't see what any girl sees in him really."

"I wouldn't exactly call six foot three little," I said, and his father's bank account isn't little either. The combination will be very attractive to some girls."

"He may be tall and wealthy but he's still a little spoiled brat. Stature is a state of mind. I'm too much of a lady to tell you what I really think of him."

"I'm sure we can guess," I said. Ross just fluttered her eyelids and smiled demurely.

"I don't think his father's bank account is part of the attraction here." Father Sean said. "Heather Leventhals' family is quite well off. In fact, the proposed marriage may be more of a business merger than a matter of the heart."

"Well, now isn't that a sad state of affairs," Ross said.

"Anyway Ladies, I must away. Ross, may I give you a lift?"

"Thank you Sean, but I'd rather walk. It's such a lovely autumn day; reminds me of Oxford when I was a girl, ...before the war. It's been lovely, and please Jo, don't hesitate o call me if you need to talk, or just to be with someone."

"I appreciate that, Ross, thank you. You too Sean. Thanks. What would one do without really good friends?" We all walked down to the street together. As I walked to my car I chucked my pack of cigarettes in a nearby trash can.

Chapter 9

Of course nothing could
happen over the weekend. I
visited Lee as often as was allowed. His
spirits seemed to be good but I was sure he was
keeping up appearances for my sake. His major
complaint, as might be expected, was the food. He
said he was always just a bit hungry and that he
would never eat another bologna sandwich again in
his life.

At home, we all kept ourselves as busy as
possible. Ben and Jay got the last of the harvest in
and were busy with the crush in the winery. I fed
animals, pulled weeds, cleaned kitchen cabinets, dried
herbs, canned tomatoes, and answered the phone; gawd,
how I answered that damn phone! It seemed like every well-
wisher and curiosity-seeker in the county called. Eventually I
quit answering, which was hard since I am a compulsive phone
answerer. Basically, I did everything but get my butt into my
desk and work on that blasted book. I just found that it was nearly
impossible to concentrate. Whenever I did sit down and work, it was
usually a waste of time. When I reread it, it was usually worthless
and had to be deleted.

Sure, I still had recipes to test, but it was damn hard to cook
creatively, particularly when the meals I cooked were eaten with a
significant lack of enthusiasm. Ben and Jay ate rather automatically.
I doubted that they tasted anything. The dogs seemed appreciative
of the fallout however.

Lee went before the judge Monday morning. The lab tests had of
course shown that the tissue under Ginger's nails was his. There
was however, tissue besides Lee's. The lab tests also determined that

the fetus was not his. Of course he pleaded not guilty. Bale was set at $100,000.00. Ben rushed to his bank, did some shuffling, produced the required 10 percent and they were both home by mid afternoon.

Lee hit the kitchen like a vacuum cleaner. He cleaned up most of the leftovers in the refrigerator, made himself two huge Dagwood sandwiches and emptied the cookie jar and the jug of milk before going upstairs to shower. Then he came back downstairs and asked if we could have pizza for dinner.

This time when the phone rang Jay answered it. "Mom, Grump, its Jason."

I snatched the phone from him. "Jason! So what's happening? What do we do next?"

"Is it all right if I come over? We can talk then."

"Of course. Come for dinner. Lee's ordered pizza."

"Sure. I'll be there in about an hour. Have a few things to clear up here at the office first."

Attorneys do not make house calls but in spite of Ben's abuses, they were good friends. Gray haired, bushy browed Jason had been one of Ben's best friends for decades. Cynic that I am, I still couldn't help but wonder if he would be charging his hourly rate while he had his feet under our table munching down on my pizza. Pizza, humm ..., speaking of which, I'd better get it out and start thawing it. O.K., O.K. So I sometimes serve frozen pizza, but that's not what you might think. I make the elements and freeze them. I always have frozen dough and sauce in the freezer. I can have a fresh pizza on the table in about half an hour: crank up the oven to 550°, thaw the dough and sauce, grate the cheeses and chop some ham or salami, scatter on some fresh diced tomatoes, mushrooms, basil and some of Ben's olives and we have a damn good pizza in minutes.

Given Lee's voracious appetite, today I made two huge ones and the large salad Lee had requested. He said he was dying for something fresh and crisp. I was just taking the pizzas out of the oven when Jason arrived. Ben went to the cellar for what he called his "everyday" red and we were ready for a decent family meal; our first in what seemed like ages. Despite my anxiety level, I tried to be a gracious hostess and not bombard Jason with questions as soon as he entered the kitchen. I was also afraid of what the answers might be.

Lee was the first to take the reins. "O.K. So what's the scoop? Am I in for it or what? I know I didn't kill Ginger, and I didn't need a damn lab report to know that the kid wasn't mine either. I just hope that all of you know it too."

"Shit Bro," Jay spat. "You don't have to ask. I didn't need a God damn DNA test to know the kid wasn't yours. I know you had better taste than to screw that piece of trash."

"Jay! I do wish you wouldn't talk like that. The poor girl's dead."

"Hell Ma. That doesn't change the fact that she was a slut."

"That's enough!" I shot.

"I think she was just really messed up," Lee said as he fiddled with a piece of pizza crust before giving it to the huge shaggy head in his lap. Immediately Alistair and George were at his side with wagging tails and hopeful expressions. "So," he turned to Jason, "where do we go from here?"

"Well," Jason began after taking a sip of his wine, "Judith McFay has agreed to represent you Lee. Believe me, she is the best in the county. Now Ben, she doesn't come cheap; and of course it will depend on whether the case goes to trial or not. I can't urge you strongly enough to retain her."

"Christ Jason! Cost isn't the issue is it?" Ben spat.

"Is it really that serious?" Lee said leaning forward, a slice of pizza half way to his mouth. "Do you really think it's necessary to hire a big booming attorney when there was someone else's tissue under her nails too and when the kid wasn't mine? Can't you do it?"

"I'm not a criminal attorney. I'm a paper shuffler. I don't think you should take chances. I really recommend you hire the best and that's Judith McFay. Call her tomorrow. She wants to talk to you as soon as possible."

"Jesus!" Lee leaned back and let out a long breath. "This really is serious then, isn't it?"

"Yes, I'm afraid it is."

"That's assholeism! To think Lee did it is down right insulting. My brother isn't stupid enough to bludgeon the girl to death and then drag her body home and stuff it in a bin of our own Zinfandel grapes."

"The D.A. will say that under strain people do irrational things, however you do have an excellent point and it's one that I'm sure Ms. McFay will stress in her defense."

"Still wish you were on the case," Ben grumbled. You've been this families' attorney for years. Hell, you're the only damn attorney I trust."

"I appreciate that Ben" he said with a chuckle, "considering all the stress you've put my heart through over the years. This however is way out of my league. I'd be doing you a great disservice if I lead you to believe that I could handle it. But I won't abandon the family. I'll help Judith in any way I can." Ben grumbled something under his breath and all the dogs rushed to his side waiting for a scratch or a bit of pizza crust.

"What about Alberto?" Lee asked. "Can she represent him too?"

"He can qualify for representation from the public defender's office."

"Lot of help that will be. He deserves the best there is too."

"Unfortunately, I don't think his family is in a position to be able to afford Judith. Anyway, it would most likely be considered a conflict of interest."

"So, what are we going to do, just sit back and let him be railroaded because he can't afford a decent attorney?"

"The people at the public defender's office are very competent. Besides, Alberto's case isn't very serious. Most of his problem is just the violation of probation over the gun."

"It still doesn't seem quit fair."

"Don't worry about Alberto. Anyway, I must leave. I have to be in court in the morning with an insurance dispute and I have a lot work yet to do to prepare, so I must go. Thanks for dinner Jo." He got up, shook hands all around and gave me a hug. When he got to the door he turned, "and don't talk to the press. Tell Alberto and his family the same. I know this sounds inane, but try not to worry."

*   *   *

We were still sitting around the kitchen table when Alistair, George and Maggie came to attention, then shot out, the screen door slamming behind them. Ben grumbled as a car crunched over the gravel on the drive. The engine stopped and a car door slammed.

"Hey! You in there! Call off your goddamn dogs! Hey you in there! I'm talkin' to you!"

"Now who the hell's that?" Ben grumbled.

Lee looked out the kitchen window. "Christ! It's Ginger's father. What's he doing here?"

"Yeh! You, Penella! Get your fat ass out here and that murdering grandson of yours too!"

Lee started for the door. "No," Ben put a hand on his arm. "You'd best stay inside." He opened the screen door and stood on the top step. "Who are you sir, and what can I do for you?" That was a shocker, given Ben's usual temperament. I'm sure it was only with the greatest effort that Ben was managing to keep his temper. I could see he was seething inside.

"I want justice! That's what I want!

"Well Sir, you're living in the right country," Ben said curtly.

"Yea..." the intruder spat. "Maybe fur you rich fucking wine sons-a-bitches but not fur us poor folks. What kind of justice let's a fucking goddamn murdering rapist and his spick buddy kill my little girl and get away with it?" He continued to rant but he came no closer. Alistair, George and Maggie, normally quite hospitable, responded to his manner by curling their lips, raising the hair on the backs of their necks and emitting throaty growls while pacing back and forth stiff-legged and threatening. Just then, he made the mistake of hurling the Jim Beam bottle he had been swigging from. It hit little Alistair. He gave out a sharp yelp of pain and fell on his side. George and Maggie simultaneously sailed through the air and were on top of him. Ben flew off the porch followed by Lee and Jay. Ben picked up Alistair's limp body and the boys joined the dogs.

55

I'm sure things would have gotten a lot worse if a pair of headlights hadn't just then come up the drive. Two uniformed officers got out of a patrol car. Jay and Lee immediately retreated towards the porch, pulling the dogs with them.

"Get them!" Ed Sloan shrieked as he staggered toward the officers. "You saw 'em! They killed my little girl, then they tried to kill me. I want justice!" He stumbled and one of the officers caught him. "Take your hands off-a me you lousy cop. Them's the ones you should be man handling," and he jerked his head towards the house.

"No one's manhandling you Sir. Now what's all this about?"

"They murdered my little girl and they're getting off scott free! That's what it's about." He staggered and fell against the side of his rusted pickup. Jay and Lee were having a hard time restraining the dogs. "Came here to get justice and they secked them vicious mutts on me. You saw... them mutts nearly killed me ... had me down ... about ripped my throat out!" One of the officers reached out a hand to steady him and he knocked it away.

"Take it easy Sir," the officer said, then over his shoulder, "I think you should put the dogs in the house."

"Why the fuck don't you do something?" Ed shouted. "You saw what them rich fuckin' bastards tried to do to me. All I want's a little fuckin' justice and respect. If you're poor you don't get no respect."

"Now calm down Sir."

"I'll fuckin' calm down when I get a little justice." With that he opened the door of the truck and attempted to climb in. "That's all I want...jus' a little fuckin' justice."

"I don't think you should be driving in your condition," the officer said.

"What the fuck d'y mean? I'll drive any where I fuckin' want..." and he reached for the steering wheel.

"Not in that condition Sir," and the officer put a restraining hand on him. With that, Ed lunged for the officer and fell out of the cab of the pickup and landed flat on his face. When the officers tried to help him up he doubled up his fist and took an ineffective punch, and that was that. The officers were on him and had him cuffed and in the back of the squad car before you could blink.

"Now then," one of them said, "I'd better come in and get a statement."

"Sure," Ben said, still cradling poor little Alistair in his arms, who had recovered and was struggling to get down and join the fray. "How did you happen to show up here when you did, anyway?"

"We had just turned onto Arnold Drive when we got a call that there was a disturbance we should check out."

"I called Allen," I said. "I was afraid you might lose your temper Ben."

"Me? Lose my temper? Why, I'm surprised at you Jo. You know I'm always in perfect control."

Chapter 10

The following morning found me up early and in the kitchen preparing for my class. Once a month I give cooking lessons to a group of women from San Francisco. Mostly they're dilettantes who aren't really all that interested in actually learning to cook. They're wealthy wives with time on their hands, who came to Sonoma each month for the quintessential "Wine Country," weekend. They stay at the Sonoma Inn, go to a spa, visit a few wineries, have dinner at a trendy restaurant and take my cooking classes.

I had considered canceling this month, figuring they would be far more interested in our tragedy than in the proper method for caramelizing onions. However, it was a bit late to cancel and besides, I could use the ladies as guinea pigs for some more Zinfandel recipes.

Today's menu would include what I called Buena Vista Meat Balls on fresh blue-cheese polenta, Aragua and fresh mushroom salad with a Zinfandel/mustard vinaigrette, served of course with the excellent sourdough bread from the Sonoma bakery on The Plaza. I make excellent bread but I have never mastered classic San Francisco sourdough. I don't have the oven for it. I decided on a late harvest Zinfandel sorbet for dessert. At the last minute, I decided to also try out an idea I had for Zinfandel brownies. Hey! Don't wrinkle up your nose. A lot of people like to eat chocolate with Zinfandel. Why not put them together.

Usually I rather enjoyed these sessions. Today however, having my kitchen filled with curiosity seekers promised no particular joy. I was taking a break, sitting on the back stoop with a cup of coffee and a cigarette watching the morning sun turn the vines to gold, when Ben joined me.

"I thought I smelled cigarette smoke. What the hell are you doing? You quit years ago."

"So, I've started again. It's either this or I'll eat everything in sight and I sure as hell don't want to start gaining weight again." I had fought the battle of the bulge all my adult life, usually winning but it was a fight hard-won.

"Well, Sweetie, I can't say as I blame you. Just don't do it in the house, and I'm sure you will be able to quit again once this is all over. You're one of the strongest people I know."

"Oh Ben," I said in utter despair, leaning my head on his shoulder. "What are we going to do? What if they don't find who really did kill poor Ginger?"

"They will Honey, they will. Don't worry...," and his voice trailed off.

"But how can I not. I'm so worried I constantly feel like I'm about to vomit. That's when I don't feel just totally numb and unreal. Sometimes it's sort of like I'm watching a surrealist movie and not liking it very much."

"It's going to all be O.K." He gave me a reassuring hug. I knew that underneath Ben was just as worried as I was.

"Oh why did Lee and Alberto have to stop off at that damn bar that night. He wouldn't be in this mess if he'd come straight home."

"Should-a, had-a, ought-a," he said and stood up wearily. "I'd best get to work. It won't do itself."

I snuffed out my cigarette and stood as well. "I'll call you when breakfast is ready."

"You've got enough on your plate this morning what with your class and all. I have to go into town in a bit. I'll just stop off someplace while I'm out.

* * *

The class had gone relatively well. It did, however feel a bit like we were all walking on eggs. The ladies refrained from asking questions but as they were leaving, one gave me an overly sympathetic hug. I was glad it was over. While busying myself with cleaning up, the events of the past several days kept running through my head like they were on automatic replay. I was wiping the last of the wine glasses to remove the spots the dishwasher always left when it hit me. "There would be something in one of our cars," I shouted out loud. I put down my dishtowel and reached for the phone.

"Allen! You have to search all of our cars."

"Jo?" came the surprised voice over the phone. "What are you talking about?"

"I'm talking about, if Lee had done it, which of course he did not, there would be some evidence of the body having been in one of our cars or the truck. You send someone over here right now to go through our cars with a fine-tooth comb. If Lee had brought the body over here there would be something in the vehicle he used; blood, hair, something. I want a team of forensic experts over here right now to... "

"Hold on Jo. I can't interfere with the investigation. Since I'm a friend of the family I've been taken off. I can't do that. Besides, don't you remember, that was done the day they discovered the body."

"Well, I want them back here. Things were very confusing that day. Lots of people milling around. They were probably distracted and it didn't seem like they took very much time doing it. I want our cars searched again to absolutely prove that Lee didn't do it."

"Not finding anything in one of you cars won't really prove that Lee didn't do it, however if they did find anything it would be pretty damaging."

"Well, they won't find anything because my son did not kill that girl and I want someone over here to do a more thorough investigation so that there is absolutely no doubt."

"I'm telling you Jo, they already searched your vehicles and further searching will achieve nothing but wasting the taxpayers money. You need to talk to Lee's attorney. She'll know what to do and I'm pretty sure she will tell you what I'm telling you. Further searching will only prove fruitless; and Jo, I can't work on the case anymore. I can however, keep you appraised of what' going on."

"Thanks a lot." I slammed down the phone. It wasn't reasonable of me to be mad at Allen. He was a good friend and he'd been a great help already. I found Judith McFay's card. Of course, she wasn't in her office. I left a message. Before I had finished cleaning the kitchen, she returned my call.

"I completely agree with you Jo. I'll call the detective in charge of the investigation and see that it's done. You hang tight. I'm surprised it hasn't been done already."

"Actually Judith, they did search our vehicles, but they didn't take very long at it and I'd feel far more comfortable if I knew they had been given a thorough going over so that it was absolutely indisputable that there was no damning evidence in any of them."

"Well Jo, I don't think searching again will be very fruitful, however if it will make you feel better I'll see what I can do. I'll get right on it and see what can be done. Way to go girl. I'll keep you informed," and she hung up. I had the distinct feeling that she was being a bit patronizing and I absolutely hate the expression, "way to go." I felt she was most likely just placating me and that nothing would happen, however, late that afternoon a team was out and giving our cars a meticulous going over. Of course they wouldn't give me any information or speak to me in anything more than prefectural grunts. They were probably pissed about having to come out again, and I can't say I really blamed them. The more I thought about it the more ridiculous it seemed. I was beginning to regret my actions and to feel quite foolish. I became panic-stricken when I watched them scrape up little bits of this and that off Ben's old truck and put them in baggies. They left and I felt certain that I had worsened things.

At dinner that evening, I told everyone about it. Ben of course said I had given the cops a chance to plant evidence. Jay said he didn't think I should play detective and Lee said it didn't matter because there was nothing to find since he hadn't done anything. I went to bed filled with regrets and thinking that Jay was right; I should have kept my big fat mouth shut and not tried to play detective. What if somehow I had worsened things? What if somehow they found something that would further incriminate Lee, innocent though I knew he was. Oh, why the hell can't you learn to keep your nose out of things Josephine?

At 2:30 in the morning, I was still awake. I had tossed and turned all night. Despite the warm and fuzzy companionship of Fritz and Marmalade, sleep evaded me so I decided to get up and make a cup of tea. It was warm so I took my tea and a cigarette and went to sit on the back stoop. Alistair, George and Maggie of course accompanied me. Fritz and Marmalade, displaying feline good sense, stayed snugly in bed. The call of an owl wafted from the distance and joined the comical croacking of the frogs in the pond. I heard Cindy moving about in her paddock. I had always enjoyed the nighttime sounds of animals.

Alistair was the first to prick up his ears, then get up and walk stiff legged towards the winery. George began emitting low throaty growls. Maggie thumped her tail and looked at me in hopes of a bit of adventure. There was a crash from inside the winery followed by a loud "Shit!" All three dogs took off like bullets and began clawing, whimpering and baying at the winery doors. George was the first to abandon the doors and race to the back side of the winery. There was a piercing cry of pain mingled with baying, barking and yapping. Then came the sound of something crashing through the undergrowth at the back of the winery, the crunch of running feet and finally the grind of an engine being coaxed into action and tires spinning out the gravel at the lower end of our drive.

I ran part way down the drive but could see only disappearing taillights and the vague shadows of the dogs giving chase.

"Whatthehell's going on?" Ben appeared on the back stoop, shotgun in hand.

"I don't know. I couldn't sleep so I made a cup of tea and came out here to have a smoke and the dogs heard something in the winery."

"Probably some gawd-damn reporter snooping around."

"What's up?" Jay said blearily. "What's all the commotion?"

Just then, the dogs came trotting back up the drive. George had something in his mouth, which he proudly dropped at Ben's feet. "Jesus," Ben said as he stooped to pick it up. "It's the seat of someone's pants."

Sure enough. It was a slobber-coated piece of faded blue denim.

Chapter 11

We decided to leave investigating the intrusion until the light of morning. The dogs were duly rewarded for their vigilance. George however, thought it unjust that Ben saw fit to take his trophy away from him.

I tossed and turned for the rest of the night. It was barely light when I decided sleep was not a viable option, so I got up and headed to the kitchen to start a pot of coffee. When I got there the coffee maker was already burbling and I could smell that someone had made toast. In the gray of early morning, I could see that the winery doors were open. I snagged a cup of coffee and headed out. Ben and the dogs were already there.

"Couldn't sleep," he said. "Thought I'd come take a look. Haven't found anything yet except some overturned cases of bottles. Looks like he came in through that back window over there and knocked the cases that were stacked there over as he climbed through. Doesn't look like it was vandalism, not unless the dogs scared him off before he could do anything."

"So, what's up? You guys find anything?" Jay stood at the door, coffee in hand. He was soon joined by his brother. Fritz and Marmalade had followed them in and were rubbing against my legs; their way of letting me know that intrusion or no intrusion, they wanted breakfast.

"Whoever it was came in through the little back window," Ben said.

Lee went to the window and examined it. "You're sure right. It's been forced too. Looks like he used a crow bar or a tire iron.

Damn, we'll have to replace the sill if we want to be able to secure the winery. The wood around the latch is splintered."

"Like we don't have enough to do this time of year," Jay muttered.

"I think we can count ourselves lucky that nothing else was damaged. The equipment seems to all be O.K. and it doesn't look like he stole anything."

"Well, it'd be a bit hard for him to make off with a couple of cases of wine through that window and with George snapping at his ass," Lee said. The image made me laugh. Ben continued making a careful inspection of all the equipment just to make sure.

We were about to leave and go have breakfast when little Alistair came out from behind an oak barrel with something in his mouth. It was a scanty pair of ladies panties. Instinctively, if unjustly, we all turned to look at Lee.

"What are you all looking at me for? I didn't put them there."

His brother came to his defense first. "Of course he didn't. Besides, the cops went through this place with a fine tooth-comb. If they'd been here they'd have found them. I think they were planted here last night."

"That would certainly explain the break in," I said.

"Mom, you'd better call Allen," Jay said.

"But he's been taken off the case."

"Still think you should call him. He can at least tell us what to do and who to talk to."

"You're probably right. I'll call him right after breakfast."

"Good thing you called Jo. Put them and the scrap of denim in separate plastic bags. Don't touch them more than you have to. I'll send someone out to get them. Looks to me like your intruder was trying to plant evidence to incriminate Lee."

"That's what we thought too, and I'm quite sure it was the girl's father. After the way he acted the other day I wouldn't put it past him."

"Yep. He's pretty over the edge. We're keeping an eye on him. And Father Sean's trying to get social services to do something about the kids. Now that Ginger's gone there's no one to look after them. The father sure doesn't. You hang in there Jo. Someone'll be out shortly to pick up those things and take a look around. There might be something that you missed."

"Thanks Allen. I know you've been taken off the case. I hope it doesn't compromise your position for me to keep calling you."

"Hell no Jo. That's what friends are suppose to be for; to help and comfort each other. You may call me any damn time you want and I'll be of whatever help I can."

"I really appreciate that Allen; and Allen, I'm so sorry about being testy with you yesterday."

"Don't sweat it Jo. I know you're under an incredible amount of stress right now."

"Allen, just knowing there's good friends out there is a big help. I feel kind of funny calling Judith McFay. I know she's an excellent attorney but she's a stranger. You and Sean and Ross are like comfortable ol' shoes. Easy to be with."

"I'm glad you're comfortable with me, but I don't know about the ol' shoe bit," and he chuckled.

"Oh Allen. You know what I mean."

"Sure Jo. I know. I'll drop buy when I can just for coffee and a chat, or better yet, take you out for a bite; just to let you get away for a bit."

"I'd like that. Thanks again Allen," and I hung up. "I'm glad Allen is such a good friend."

"I think he wants to be more than just a good friend Mom," Jay said with a grin.

"Ahhh...! Don't be silly. We've been buddies for years. He's a good family friend. Nothing more. Anyway, I think he's got a bit of a crush on Charley."

"Guys don't usually stay best friends with a woman for years unless they're interested."

"Or gay," Lee added.

"I don't know about that," Ben said. "Look at Ross and me. We've been good friends for decades. Nothing more; just good friends."

"Yah, Grump," Jay said, "but that's different, isn't it."

"And just why the hell is it different?" Ben retorted with an edge of frost to his voice.

"Well, you know...different."

"What you mean young man, is that because we are both old farts we couldn't possibly be interested in anything more than friendship. Well let me tell you young man..."

"I know! I know!" Jay said throwing up both hands. "There may be snow on the roof but there's still smoke in the chimney..."

"Ah for Christ's sake...Kids! Smart ass, know-it all-kids! Get your butts in gear and meet me in the winery. Work won't do itself you know," and he stomped out followed by Alistair, George and Maggie.

"You shouldn't be rude to your grandfather, Jay."

"Ah Ma. I was just giving him the business. He likes it. Good to get him riled now and then. Keeps his brain active."

"His brain is more active than most folks half his age; and don't call me Ma."

"Sure Ma, and he scooted out the door before the oven mitt I hurled at him could make contact.

It was late afternoon and I'd put in a good day at my desk when Allen called back. "I just want to let you know the results of turning out your vehicles."

"And..." I said apprehensively.

"Well, they found blood both on the dash and in the bed of Ben's old truck..."

"Do I want to hear the rest of this?"

"Don't fret. The blood in the bed of the truck turned out to be pig. Guess you were hauling some critter... and that on the dash was Lee's which pretty much verifies his story about having scraped his knuckles when he and Alberto were working on the ol' clunker. Why the hell doesn't Ben get rid of that thing anyway?"

"Oh thank God, Allen. Does this mean that the charges will be dropped now?"

"Probably not for a while yet. It will be up to the D.A. but I don't think he seriously feels he has a case against either Lee or Alberto. Think he's just covering his butt for the press. Since there aren't any other suspects as yet, he has to look like he's making some progress in the case. I don't think you have much to worry about."

"That's damn easy for you to say. He's not your kid."

"I know Jo. Platitudes are easy for an outsider. Of course you can't help but be worried sick; but hang in there. It's got to work out. The D.A. isn't going to make an ass of himself going to court with such flimsy evidence; particularly not against Judith McFay."

Chapter 12

We were all enjoying a welcome respite from our family crisis...predicament...disaster...adventure; whatever you choose to call it. The O'Malley Zinfandel Harvest Festival was fast upon us, and this was always a much looked-forward-to occasion. Father Sean and his sister Deirdre opened their home, grounds and the winery to damn near all of Sonoma County. You were likely to find most anyone there; people in the wine industry of course, everyone from other vintners, wine makers and wine brokers, to those who worked in the vineyards and those who wrote about wine. There might be bankers and politicians, local business people and celebrities. Of course the O'Malleys considered them all to be celebrities. Their creed was that a celebrity was one who was celebrated and since they celebrated all their guests... and the occasion also celebrated the harvest and paid homage to their ancestors, the Zinfandel grape and to the earth which granted them the bounty. Father Sean always set up an altar under an arbor and celebrated a Thanksgiving Mass. All in all it was an event that was eagerly looked forward to by the entire community.

Food? Oh yeah! The O'Malley kitchen would have been a beehive of activity all week. Father Sean's mother and sister and several other women they hired for the occasion turned out mountains of delectable dishes, an eclectic collection of dishes from their composite ethnic background: Irish, Hungarian and Mexican. There would be huge meat pies, tamales, savory herb and garlic laden Paprikash liberally laced with red wine, flans, sweet rolls and mountains of crusty homemade breads.

And that wouldn't be all. Many of their friends would use the event as an excuse to show off some favorite dish of their own creation. Alberto's mother could always be counted on to bring chicken mole and homemade tamales, you can never have too many good tamales. Charley usually brought two of her outstanding cheesecakes and Mrs. Collin-Bennett supplied her delectable Cornish pasties. Despite her sophisticated upper-class English upbringing, she was of good basic Cornish stock on her mother's side. You were likely to find anything from home made pizza and pasta to sushi and BBQ, most of it good.

Of course, there would be wine, excellent wines, and not just the O'Malleys. Most of the guests who were vintners would bring samplings of their own creations to show off; and a local brew pub always supplied two kegs of a special run ale just for the occasion. I was going to use the O'Malleys' guests as guinea pigs for more Zinfandel recipes. All in all the feasting would be a far cry from what is usually deemed appropriate for a wine tasting, but then this was an exuberant celebration, not a sedate wine tasting.

It may sound a bit inappropriate to be looking forward to attending such an occasion given current events, but quite frankly, it was just what we all needed; a breather, a bit of time to be able to put it all aside and clear our minds. I just hoped that most of the people there would be good enough friends, or if not, at least polite enough not to pump us for information.

It was the morning of the Harvest Festival when Lacey called. She was excited about attending the Harvest Festival and wanted to know what would be appropriate to wear.

"Honey," I said. "You would be appropriate in anything from a thong bathing suit to a Dior evening gown. If you opt for the thong I suggest you bring a change for when you finish swimming because it can get breezy in the late afternoon."

"Me, in a thon? I don't think so."

From what I remembered of her short, stocky build, she was probably right.

"So, a sun dress or slacks would be O. K.?"

"You are going to see everything from ripped Levis and leather jackets to minks. This is one of the most eclectic gatherings you are ever likely to attend; sort of like opening night of the San Francisco opera season."

"What do you mean? Everyone dresses for the opera."

"Local joke. Just don't worry. Wear what you will be comfortable in. I particularly suggest that you wear comfortable shoes. The dancing usually goes well past midnight."

"There'll be dancing?"

"Most assuredly."

"Oh wonderful. What type of music?"

"Well, one never knows. It all depends on who shows up. Anyone who can play an instrument will bring it. There may be anything from Mariachi to rock; and there's almost always traditional Irish music. Don't worry about it. Just come and enjoy yourself."

"I was wondering if you thought it would be O.K. if I brought a salad."

"Of course it would be just fine. Lacey, don't worry about anything. The important thing is just to come and have one hell of a good time."

*   *   *

The weatherman was cooperating. It was one of those magnificent golden autumn days. A day to make you glad you're alive. The O'Malley home, an ancient adobe (well, ancient by west coast standards) gleamed in the soft autumn sunlight. It rambled along the crest of a gentle rise. Father Sean's grandfather had strategically placed it so that he could survey his holdings from the verandas that wrapped around three sides.

Sean had once told me that his grandfather was determined to build in the style of a thatched roofed Irish cottage. His wife, however, who was thoroughly steeped in her "Los Californios" heritage, had managed to convince him that such a structure was inappropriate in California's Mediterranean climate, so he had opted for adobe with the classic red tile roof. Old and gnarled grape vines clung to the verandas providing the house protection from the fierce Sonoma summer sun and venerable olives shaded the walk ways and patios. The home and winery were on the National register of historic places. The swimming pool, which Father Sean's father had added, was surrounded by more olives and grape arbors and was artfully placed so that it did not detract from the home's original charm.

As we arrived, the music of fiddle, flute and bodhrán drifted among the olives and along the walkways. Mrs. Collin-Bennett arrived as we did. Ben went to find Father Sean who was most likely overseeing the barbeque pits. The delicious smell of the roasting kids; there was always roasted kid, filled the air. I assumed that Ben was also anxious to test the quality of this year's brew pub contribution. Lee and Jay helped Ross and me carry our contributions into the kitchen before wandering off to discover what this year's crop of sweet young things had to offer.

The huge old-fashioned kitchen was a beehive of activity. Deirdre was putting the finishing touches on trays of roasted peppers, marinated artichoke hearts and pickled mushrooms. Ben had delivered a crock of his olives the day before and they stood in large wooden bowls, waiting to meet their demise. Alberto's mother presided over huge steamers filled with tamales, while Mrs. O'Malley basted the turkeys, an old family recipe from her Mexican heritage that boasted a stuffing of cornbread and chorizo and a sweet and hot chili glaze. The kitchen was filled with delectable smells and jolly chatter.

"And you two get to turn all of that into guacamole," Deirdre said as she pointed Ross and I in the direction of a huge pile of avocados, chilies, onions, tomatoes, limes and cilantro. "Here's the recipe. It's Alberto's Mom's," and she handed us a dog-eared and yellowed slip of paper.

"This certainly seems like an inordinate amount of guacamole," Ross said, eyes watering as she minced onions.

"Oh, that's just the beginning." Deirdre laughed. "Mama insists that it always be fresh. We'll be back in here 3 or 4 times to make more before the day's over."

"Hmmm....   Imagine that," Ross said with pursed lips.   Her British taste buds had made many adjustments during her decades of living in California.   Avocados, in general and Guacamole, in particular were not among them.

"How are you holding up, Jo? Deirdre asked. "I know I should have come over but what with the harvest and getting ready for this shindig..."

"Well, I can't say it's been a bed of roses, but I think things will work out.   Allen is pretty sure the charges will be dropped. He's given me a lot of support through all this."

"I sure as hell would like to know who did do it. We all know it couldn't have been Lee or Alberto either," she added after seeing Mrs. Mendez's back stiffen.

"It was probably a drifter," one of the other ladies helping Mrs. O'Malley said.

"But a drifter would have just left her; not stuff her in a box of grapes," another helper offered.

"Yes, but..."

"Thankfully, Ross, realizing neither Alberto's mother nor I were comfortable with the conversation, intervened. "Hand me another bunch of that nasty green weed you all seem to enjoy so," she said, indicating the pile of cilantro. "I don't see how you people can abide it. It tastes like soap, and not a very good soap at that." We all laughed and she continued with her diversionary tactics. "I wonder whose Zinfandel will take the gold medal at this years county fair."

"Zinfandel! Zinfandel! That's all I've heard since I moved here!." It was Lacey Coleman. She had just arrived and was standing in the doorway holding a small salad bowl. "I was told I should bring this in here, but it certainly looks like I'm carrying coals to Newcastle."

"All contributions gratefully accepted," Deidre said as she took the bowl. "Oh, ... my ... doesn't that look lovely," she said Thank you so much," and she set it on one long counter among the other contributions.

"Yes, it's a specialty of my mother's: three bean salad." I worked hard to restrain a smile as I glanced at the unremarkable offering. "And it's so easy to make," she continued. Just a can of green beans, a can of kidney beans, and a can of garbanzo beans, and some mayonnaise. The original recipe had onions and parsley but I always leave them out. So many people don't like them." Deidre and I shot each other glances and hid our smiles. I do add some of those bacon bits that come in a jar," she added. Alberto's mother let out a snort.

"Well it looks just lovely dear," Ross said and shot me a quick glance that said, "Behave yourself."

"Thank you Ross ... I hope you don't mind if I call you Ross. Mrs. Collin-Bennett is a bit of a mouthful."

"Of course dear."

"Everyone at home always begged me to bring my bean salad," she continued. "Now please, what is all this fuss about Zinfandel? You started to tell me when I was at your house Jo, and then you were interrupted."

"I'll defer to Deidre or Mrs. O'Malley. After all, they're in the family so to speak."

"What family?"

"Oh gee...where to begin?" Deidre said as she expertly cut a dozen mushroom and spinach quiches into small slices. "Have you heard of Agoston Haraszthy?"

"Not until I moved to Sonoma. Now I've heard the name, but I have no idea who he is. Father Sean told me a bit when I was at dinner at Jo's house, but I'd love to hear more."

"Actually it's was. He was an Hungarian who came here in the mid 1850's and founded the Buena Vista winery. About the only wines being made in California at that time were sacramental wines made from grapes planted by the mission padres. Old Agoston was sure California could do better so he made a trip back to Europe to collect cuttings from premium wine grapes. He managed to get cuttings from some of the best vineyards in France, Italy and Germany and bring them back to California where he planted them. He is usually credited with having founded the premium wine industry in California. He and General Vallejo became close friends and two of his sons married two of Vallejo's daughters here in the Sonoma mission. They were close friends as well as rivals. Every year they competed at the State Fair for gold medals for their wines. You see, Vallejo made wine as well."

"Golly, he must have made a fortune, being here so early and getting all that land."

"Not really. He was a brilliant and innovative man but not particularly wise and he had absolutely no head for finance. He eventually lost everything here in Sonoma. Then he thought he could make his fortune by opening a sugar plantation in Nicaragua. According to legend, he fell into a river and was eaten by a crocodile."

"You're pulling my leg."

"Nope. That's the accepted story."

"So, what did Jo mean when she said you were family?"

"My great-grandfather came here from county Kerry in Ireland in the late 1800's. The family story goes that when he stepped off the boat in San Francisco he didn't have a penny to his name, but that a month later he left San Francisco with a fine horse and a sizable bank roll and that several Barbary Coast gamblers were significantly lighter of pocket and one without his horse.

"You're kidding."

"Nope, that's the family story. He rode up here to Sonoma and charmed his way into invitations to some of the best homes including the Vallejo's where he met and wooed one of the beautiful young daughters of the Vallejo/Haraszthy union."

"He was a dreadful old rake and sinner and we shouldn't be so proud of him," Mrs. O'Malley said with a snort as she carved the roasted turkeys and piled the meat on platters.

"Now Mama, if it wasn't for that sinful old rake we wouldn't be enjoying our very pleasant lifestyle." This was answered with another snort as Mrs. O'Malley slammed more meat onto the platters.

"But what about Zinfandel?"

"Now that is as much legend as it is fact."

"Oh?"

"Zinfandel had never been known before it appeared at Buena Vista after Haraszthy came back from his European collecting trip. Where it came from and how it got its name no one can say for sure. Some say that it is the result of a mutation of one of the cuttings that Haraszthy brought back. Some say the name is the missspelling of the Austrian "Zierfandler," and others say it is of the Vinifera family. We like to think that it is a California phenomenon; however, there are those who claim that it was being grown in other parts of the U.S. as early as 1832. Myth or no myth there is no getting around the fact that when properly made it's an excellent and distinctive wine with a dedicated following."

"What about white Zinfandel?"

To this, Mrs. O'Malley gave another loud snort and then spat, "An absolute abomination!"

"Now Mama... it has it's place. Let's just say its wine with training wheels."

To this, Mrs. O'Malley muttered something under her breath and set about ladling Paprikash into huge bowls.

Just then, Father Sean entered the kitchen. "The kids are about done," he said
"and everything's ready for Mass. Are things about ready in here?"

Chapter 13

A veritable army of volunteers appeared to help carry the food to the long trestle table that had been set up out by the BBQ, Jay among them. I shot Jay a stern scowl as I saw him try to purloin a Cornish pasty. Lee was still playing fiddle with the group of Irish musicians.

If you have ever wondered what a groaning board really looks like, this was it. The well-worn natural wood of the tabletop was barely visible under the cascade of victuals. The staggering array of dishes was interspersed with crusty golden loaves of Mrs. O'Malley's home baked bread. Grape vines and fat clusters of grapes were intertwined through all.

Four kids and two lambs, their skins crispy and golden brown, sizzled as they turned on their spits. Ben was taking a turn as bartender, dispensing paper cups of this year's special brew and a wide assortment of wines, his own included.

Father Sean, with two of Alberto's young siblings acting as acolytes, stepped to the altar which had been set up under an arbor. The music stopped and we all became quiet as he performed his traditional Thanksgiving Mass, during which he welcomed everyone, thanked them for coming and sharing in his family's good fortunes. He gave thanks for the bountiful harvest, blessed the new wine and the food and after, invited anyone for whom it was appropriate to take communion.

Someone began playing a Celtic harp and the guests began milling about the table, helping themselves to the array of dishes. Father Sean and Alberto began carving the spitted lambs and kids. Much to their delight, he handed his two young acolytes each a leg bone, with lots of meat still on them. They scampered off, greedily ripping at the succulent meat with their teeth while their mother chased them, warning them not to get the grease on their good clothes. Then she came back and chided Father Sean for allowing them to be greedy little pigs.

"It's a feast day," he said. "Let them be; and there's nothing wrong with a little dirt."

"Good. Then tomorrow I bring their clothes for you to wash, Father," and she stomped off as Sean laughed and continued carving.

His attention was averted when he felt a tug at his sleeve. Looking down he saw the large brown eyes of one of Alberto's little sisters. "Please, Father," she whispered. "Can I have the piggy's tail?"

"I don't know, little one, can you?"

"Sowey," she said hanging her head, "I mean may I have the piggy's tail?"

"Of course you may," he said chopping off the tail of one of the pigs, wrapping it in a napkin and handing it to her. She took it, thanked him and skipped off chewing on the crispy skin.

The harpist set her instrument aside to join the queue at the table and a Mariachi band replaced her.

Ben was relieved as bartender. He and father Sean were engaged in conversation with the rep from a major wine distributor and the wine editor of a local newspaper joined them. "How long do you plan on leaving this year's crush on the oak?" the rep asked Sean.

"Do you predict this year's Zin will have the characteristic brambly quality?" asked the editor.

"These are all questions you should be asking Deirdre. She's the one who went to viniculture school at Davis. I went to seminary school. It's a rather nice arrangement. She uses her knowledge of art and science and I ask God to help her. She makes the wine and I bless it."

The editor turned to Ben, "How long do you plan on leaving your Zin on the oak this year?" he asked.

"I don't tell the wine," Ben answered. "The wine tells me."

"Your Zins usually have the delightful characteristic brambly quality with overtones of spice," the rep said swirling his glass and taking a sip.

"I feel the Penella Zins show a significant concentration of purity and depth, with just enough vigor to give them a fragrant nose; exotic, compelling..."

"Precisely," said the owner of a cheese and wine shop on the plaza, who had just joined the group. "The Penella wines are bold, yet graceful...the result of the cooler climate from the east-facing slopes...a hint of strawberry and cherry..."

"Ah, and I definitely detect the dark earthy undertones of nutmeg and chocolate, exotic, truly exotic..."

"Mmmm, and that touch of pepper ads a bit of mischief."

"Now as for Ben's Chardonnay, those subtle flinty undertones..."

"Bollix!" Ben snorted and spat his wine on the ground. "Bollix! When was the last time you licked a piece of flint or chewed on a bramble bush? My wines don't taste like flint or bushes. I don't use nutmeg or chocolate. If I wanted a wine that tasted like strawberries or cherries I'd make strawberry or cherry wine. My wines taste like wine! Damn good wine! And if you don't know the difference between chocolate, pepper, flint, bramble bushes and wine, then what the hell business do you have writing about wine or selling it. Grow up furchristsakes!" And he stomped off to the bar and pulled himself a pint of ale.

The "wine experts" were left looking at each other with open mouths. The shop owner was the first to recover. "Old Ben is such a character. It's no wonder his wines are so distinctive."

"Yes," said the editor. "That's Ben for you. It's easy to see where his wines get their bold and distinctive..."

Sean could hardly keep from laughing. He managed to say, "If you will excuse me, I need to check on the BBQ." When he caught up with Ben he slapped him on the back and laughed heartily. "Well, so much for wine talk."

"Aaa... all that malarkey gives me a pain in the ass. You know there isn't a wine in the world that tastes like pepper or flint or Cherries Jubilee! Jerks! Cork Dorks!"

"Hell, Ben. As long as you've been in the business you ought to have learned by now to let them play their little games. When Bernard Shaw said, "those who can, do and those who can't, teach," he could have just as easily said, "those who can make wine, do make wine, and those who can't, write about it. You and Deirdre make wine, let the others play their game. Besides, they do help sell it."

Having overheard the set-to with the "experts," I couldn't help but wince, for as a food and wine writer, I was just a bit guilty of using some rather, ... hmmmm, "flowery" adjectives to describe the fruit of the vine as well.

Ben was waving his pint of ale about and pontificating on some political issue when Rod Gardino, Sr. sidled up to him and clapped a hand on his shoulder.

"So, Ben, Ol' Man, when are you going to sell me that old run down place of yours?"

"When you grow a dick. You've already got more balls than you need."

Gardino, Sr. rubbed his chin in a rather smarmy fashion. "Crusty ol' bastard, aren't you. But come now, Ben. Let's face it. You aren't getting any younger. You could..."

Ben cut him short with a roar of indignation. "What the hell are you talking about?" Ben's outburst caused all conversation in the immediate area to come to a halt and all heads to turn.

"I mean, Ol' Man, it's time you thought about taking it easy. I'll give you a damn good price, considering the condition the place is in. You could take the money, invest, get a nice little condo someplace and enjoy yourself."

"I am enjoying myself and what the hell do you mean, 'the condition of the place'?"

"Well, face it, Ben, there's no value in that ramshackle collection of buildings. I'll just have to bulldoze them to make room for more grapes. And the olives and other fruit trees will have to go. They don't produce anything of market value. Pulling them out will be expensive and..."

Ben was now spluttering with rage, unable to articulate an understandable word. Gardino continued, "If you utilized the land properly you wouldn't be in a position to have to sell..."

"You can take your bulldozer, your utilization and your mafia backing and stuff it up your worthless ass. What the hell do you mean, 'in a position to have to sell,' you right wing Fascist bastard."

I could see people murmuring to each other and passing questioning looks.

"Face it Ben, that antiquated operation of yours can't be netting you much and what with all your current expenses and problems...well, I'm just trying to be neighborly and help you out, that's all. "Face it, you..."

"If you say 'face it,' one more time I'll give you something to face, you sonofabitch. I ought to punch you right in your big fat Dego nose." That was a bit funny since Ben was half-Italian. "Neighborly my ass. You've been trying to buy up the whole valley ever since you moved here. It's like something out of a B-run western you slug-sucking buzzard-fucker!"

This brought quite a round of laughter from the bystanders. "Ol' Ben never was much for mincing words," I heard someone behind me say.

"It's just with all your current problems and expenses..." Gardino continued.

"My problems are my business and I'll thank you to keep your nose out of it. You've been like a blight ever since you and that damn worthless brat of yours moved into the valley. I'll tell you what you do... go stick your head up your ass and the rest of us'll shove you in all the way and your kid behind you. Smooth talking, womanizing pimp." Ben's face was now the color of a beet, which made the little tufts of gray hair above each ear look all the whiter.

Father Sean put a restraining hand on Ben's shoulder. "Ben, don't rile yourself. We need help tapping a new keg," and he led Ben away towards the bar.

Ed Gardino straightened the lapels of his shiny suit. "We'll just have to wait and see what happens," he called after Ben.

"In a rat's ass you fore-flushing, right-wing shyster," Ben called over his shoulder as Sean continued to steer him towards the bar.

"You tell em', Grump," I heard Lee shout. He had joined Ben and

Sean at the bar and was helping with the keg.

"The old man's loony,... dangerous," Gardino said to the group of bystanders. "You all saw him threaten me. He's incompetent." He turned to me. "Jo, you ought to have him put away. You're a smart little lady. You can see he doesn't know what he's doing. You come to me and I'll make a fair offer for that ol' place."

I simply gave him an icy stare, turned my back and walked away. The crowd started to disperse. "Well, now wasn't that lovely," Ross said. "What a thoroughly unpleasant man. I wonder that he was invited."

"Oh he's never invited," Deirdre said. "He just shows up in hopes of making contacts and that kid of his tries to make conquests with all the girls. Last year Sean caught him in the winery with a fifteen year old. He had her behind one of the casks trying to seduce her. She was in tears. I thought Sean was going to strangle him."

With the impromptu entertainment over for the moment, people drifted off to replenish their drinks or graze at the now-decimated food tables. As evening approached, the lanterns strung across the patios and pool and among the olive trees came on. Most of the young people went off to the barn where a small rock group was playing. The fiddle, flute and bodhrán struck up again on the patio.

Mrs. O'Malley and her helpers began tidying up the buffet tables; taking away empty platters, consolidating dishes and replenishing the more popular ones. I noticed that there wasn't a crumb of a Cornish pasty in site. Lacey's small bowl of three-bean salad however was virtually untouched. I looked around to see if anyone was watching and pondered on dumping most of it into one of the trash bags so that her feelings wouldn't be hurt. I had the bowl in my hands and was just about to dump it when I saw her walking towards me. Instantly I snatched up a paper plate and scraped a large portion of the salad onto it.

"I just had to come back for seconds," I said as she approached me. "It's so good. I must get the recipe from you."

"Oh I'm so glad you like it Jo," she smiled. "All this food is so ... interesting. You people here in California certainly do have ... unusual tastes in food. Why I have absolutely no idea what most of it is ... and so much garlic and onion. I suppose I'll get used to it."

"Yes, I suppose you will," I said taking a mouth full of her salad. "It's either that or starve."

Jay had come back to the table in hopes of finding an overlooked Cornish pasty and came to my rescue. "Hay Mom, save me of that for me," and he snagged the plate from my hands and headed back to the dancing in the winery where I knew it would wind up in a trash can.

I smiled at Lacey. "He saved me from myself. Calories you know," and I patted my hips.

While those in the winery were "rocking out," others were dancing jigs and reels to the traditional Irish music on the patio. A few were still swimming by lantern light. Ben was holding fourth at the taps, animatedly explaining the atrocities of corporate greed to a bemused audience when the night was suddenly shattered; rent asunder by a shot. A large blue glazed ceramic planter on the patio shattered into fragments. There was a split second of dead silence, followed by chaotic screeches and screams and rushing feet. Then two more shots in rapid succession and Father Sean who had rushed towards the patio fell to the ground.

"You rich fuckin' bastards! Rich mother-fuckin' wine bastards think you can do anything you want and get away with it!" Ed Sloan stood in the shadows of an old olive tree. "Well I'm here to see that you don't get away with it!" he screamed. He took a final pull from a bottle of whiskey, tossed it aside and waving a small hand gun in a large ark as he swayed back and forth, he fired three more shots. Two of them ripped through the evening air and landed harmlessly among the olive trees. The third found a more fragile mark. A young woman carrying a tray of dirty glasses across the patio screamed, then fell to the paving stones, surrounded by a shower of shattered glass.

He continued to wave his gun in the air. "You mother-fuckin' bastards up here having a good time while my little girl is dead and one of you sons o' bitches killed her. You sons o' bitches killed my baby. My beautiful baby..."

We all stood stark frozen for a fraction of a moment. Then Mrs.

O'Malley and several others ran towards Father Sean, who was sitting on the ground holding his leg. Others rushed to the woman. "Stay where you are," Ed Sloan shrieked. "None of you fuckers move," and he shot again. Nothing happened. When the gun didn't fire several men rushed him. He tried holding them off using the butt of the gun as a bludgeon. His efforts were ineffective. He was too drunk and the gun too small. They overpowered him and held him on the ground, kicking and screaming.

One of the guests who had rushed and knelt beside the fallen woman, stood and said, "I think she's dead. Oh God! I think she's dead."

Lacey, it turned out, before she decided to move to California to open the art gallery, had been a nurse. She knelt beside the woman for a moment, then removed her light linen jacket and placed it over the woman's head. She stood and walked quietly away, sat on a bench, took a pack of cigarettes from her pocket and lit one. I sat down beside her and took one as well.

The wail of sirens could be heard winding up the road. Four squad cars, two ambulances, and Allen's unmarked car arrived. Allen had been on call and not able to attend the event. Ed was cuffed and shoved shrieking into one of the squad cars. Father Sean was placed on a stretcher and taken to one of the ambulances. "He'll be fine," a paramedic assured Mrs. O'Malley and Deirdre. "It's just a leg wound. Once they get the bullet out there won't be anything to worry about. It doesn't look like it got even near the bone." Mrs. O'Malley was in hysterics and Father Sean asked if I could stay with her and Deidre. I said of course I would, however, Mrs. O'Malley could not be dissuaded from riding in the ambulance with him.

The body of the dead woman was placed in the other ambulance. As it drove away, Jay came wandering out of the winery with his arm around the shoulder of a young woman. "Hey! What the hells going on? Are those cop cars? What's the ambulance for? What gives?"

"Oh Christ," I said. "Of course with that damn music playing so loud you didn't hear the shots or sirens."

"What shots? What sirens?"

"Ginger's father showed up drunk off his ass and started shooting up the place." I offered up a little silent thanks that both my boys had been safely insulated in the winery with the music.

"Anyone hurt?"

"I'm afraid so," I said. "One of Mrs. O'Malley's helpers is dead and Father Sean was shot in the leg."

"Father Sean!"

"Don't worry," I said. "It's just a flesh wound in the leg. He'll be fine once they get the bullet out."

While I was talking to Jay, Allen, Ben and an officer went into the winery. In a few minutes the music stopped. Since no one in the winery had heard or seen anything, those with their own transportation were asked to leave. The rest were asked to stay in the winery until the officers had finished questioning the other guests who were asked to assemble on the large patio.

"Who called 911?" a young officer asked. Three people stood up. They had used their cell phones. "We'll begin with the three of you then," he said, and the tedious process of questioning the guests began.

Chapter 14

The ungracious sun shown into my room with unpleasant disregard. We hadn't arrived home until dawn. After Allen and his minions had finished questioning everyone, we stayed to help Deirdre with the cleanup.

I could hear Ben downstairs in the kitchen. "Shit!" I said to myself as I glanced at the clock. "It's only 8:15. We didn't get home until six for Christ's sake." I don't know how he does it. It's like the man doesn't need sleep at all. I threw the blankets over my head in an attempt to block out the infernal light and tried to burrow my way back to sleep. Not only was I still tired, but I wanted to hold the day at bay as long as possible. I wanted to avoid the phone calls, the questions, the curiosity seekers and most likely even the press. I remained in denial for a few minutes. "Shit, Jo!" my conscience said, "Don't be such a selfish bitch. Deirdre and her mother will be going through hell this morning and you promised Sean you'd help them." I threw back the covers, sat up and resigned myself to the fact that I would have to face the day at some point. It might as well be now, so I drug myself into the shower, dragged on a pair of Levis and a turtle-neck and went downstairs. Ben had fresh hot coffee, O.J. and French toast waiting. Lee and Jay came down shortly after me. They looked no better than I felt.

Ben, on the other hand, was disgustingly awake, though his mood was somber. "Don't rush yourselves to take care of the animals," he said as he put plates of French toast in front of each boy and slammed the pitcher of syrup on the table. "I've done it."

"Sorry Grump," Jay mumbled.

"Yea, me too," Lee added.

"I don't see how you do it Ben," I said as I poured myself a cup of coffee. You were up just as late as we were."

"At my age I don't like to waste what time I have left laying in bed. I guess time changes its perspective depending on whether most of it's ahead of you or behind you. You may feel you have time to squander. I certainly don't." He poured himself another cup of coffee and glowered into it. "Forgive me," he said. "I guess I'm in a very bad mood. I have no right to take it out on the rest of you. Enjoy your breakfast boys. I couldn't sleep so I got up and did the chores before coming into the kitchen."

"Oh Ben ... no apologies needed," I said getting up from my chair to give him a hug. "We're all out of sorts this morning. Does anyone know who the woman who was killed was?

"Alberto told me she was a friend of his mother's," Jay said. "They both work for Mrs. O'Malley sometimes."

"Did she have family?"

"Yes, according to Alberto, she's a single mom with a bunch of kids."

"How tragic."

"It's God-damned unfair," Ben mumbled into his coffee mug. "Well, hurry along guys. We've a lot to do today. You're going over to the O'Malley's, Jo?"

"Yes, they'll need help and I promised Sean I would."

When I arrived at the O'Malley's, Mrs. O'Malley, Ross and Alberto's mother were in the big kitchen drinking coffee as they went about the business of finishing the cleanup. Alberto's mother was at the sink and Ross was folding a mountain of kitchen linens, fresh out of the dryer. When her old ringer-washer had finally died last year, Mrs. O'Malley had finally acquiesced to using the automatic washer and dryer that Sean bought her. Prior to that she had hung a huge wash each and every morning. Sean told me he was sure she liked them despite the fact that she constantly complained that the laundry didn't smell nice like it did when you hung things on a line. She still insisted on hanging her best table linens, not trusting them to any modern contrivance. Her eyes were swollen and red-rimmed this morning, but despite the trauma of the previous night, she was scrubbed, brushed and dressed as immaculately as ever, and the kitchen smelled of coffee and fresh baked goods. Being a lady of the old school, come hell or high water, she was in harness by 6:00 a. m., either in her kitchen or her garden. I saw that the kitchen phone had been unplugged.

Ross saw that I noticed. "It had been ringing itself frantic. I thought it best just to silence the bloody thing."

"Probably a good idea. Where's Deirdre?" I asked as I poured myself a cup of coffee.

"She went to the hospital to pick up Sean," Ross said.

"How is he?"

Just then we heard a car come up the drive and a car door slam. A few moments later Father Sean hobbled into the kitchen on crutches, followed by Deirdre.

"Oh Son!" Mrs. O'Malley exclaimed and rushed across the room to him.

"Careful Mom," don't knock me over. I'm not to stable on these things yet.

"Oh Son! Thank goodness, you're all right. I'll get you coffee. Have you had breakfast? Would you like some eggs and chorizo? Pancakes? Hot biscuits?"

"No Mom, I'm fine. I had breakfast in the hospital."

Mrs. O'Malley gave a derogatory snort. "You call that breakfast? Sit down." She poured him coffee and went to the stove.

"You don't look too much the worse for wear," I said. "So, how are you?"

"I'll know after I have a decent cup of coffee," he said plopping down in a kitchen chair with his leg stretched out in front. He propped his crutches against the table and took a swallow from the ceramic mug Mrs. O'Malley had filled for him. "Even though it was only over night, it was still a hospital and I hate them. I even hate them when I'm visiting a parishioner."

Mrs. O'Malley went to the stove and Alberto's mother poured more coffee for us all before returning to the sink and the mountain of dirty pots and pans left from the night before. Ross continued folding the kitchen linens. Deirdre went to the pantry, returned with a bottle of brandy and generously laced Sean's coffee.

"Thanks Sis," he said with a smile, and then with a groan he shifted his bandaged let.

"So," I prodded. "How is that thing?" and I indicated his leg with my raised coffee mug.

"It's not serious. The bullet went straight through. Didn't hit the bone or even do too much tissue damage. They only kept me overnight because of the amount of blood I lost. I had to have a transfusion."

Just then a police officer stuck his head in the open kitchen door. "We've finished up so we'll be going now. Oh, good morning, Father. How ya feelin'?"

"Pretty good now that I'm away from the hospital and the stump water they call coffee."

The officer laughed, "Glad it wasn't too serious." Then turning to Mrs. O'Malley, "The boys said to thank you for the coffee and fresh rolls. We'll be going now." He left and we heard the squad car crunch down the gravel drive.

I couldn't believe it. Despite everything that had happened ,Mrs. O'Malley had been up at dawn making coffee and hot rolls for the police. I had no idea just how old she was but given that Sean was pushing fifty with a short stick, she must have been seventy or thereabouts. Deirdre was considerably younger. There had been a brother between Sean and Deirdre who had been killed in Vietnam.

Sean shifted his leg again with a grimace, took a healthy swallow of coffee, and unfolded the Sunday paper Deidre had picked up on their way home from the hospital. The events of the previous night had shoved the war in the Middle East, gas prices and the bombings of Planned Parenthood centers off the front page. There was a large photo of Ed Sloan being taken out of the squad car in front of the Sonoma County Adult Facility and a picture of Ginger smiling seductively.

"Priest Shot by Father of Pregnant Girl,"

the headline screamed.

We were dumb struck. Mrs. O'Malley began to cry.

"Why, they made it sound like Sean fathered that girl's baby," Ross said with British indignation.

Deirdre picked up the phone. Finding it dead she impatiently plugged it in and asked information for the number of the editorial desk of the local paper. She dialed, held the receiver to her ear for a moment, then slammed the receiver down in rage. "Damn it! It's Sunday. Can't get through to a human."

"Don't fret Deirdre," Sean tried to soothe. "It's all explained in the article."

"You know damn well that most Americans don't read articles! They just read headlines!"

"Sean, Deirdre," I said. "Perhaps you should call the media and offer a press meeting and give them the entire story."

"Good idea," Deirdre said and picked up the phone again. Then slammed it down again. "Crap. It's still Sunday isn't it?" she laughed. "Of course, our marvelous 'Podunk Currier' doesn't man the phones on weekends."

Sean continued to scan the paper. Buried on page six, he found a small article about the woman who had been killed. It showed a picture of her six children and told how she was a widow, her husband having been killed in an automobile accident.

"What a tangled mess," Ross said. "This is certainly an example of the domino effect isn't it?"

"How jou mean?" asked Galena, Alberto's mother.

"Well," Ross said, as she continued folding the linens, "Just look at all the lives that have been touched because of that girls death. First, poor Ginger is killed, thus bringing grief to her family. Then Alberto is implicated, which puts your family in jeopardy, and Jo's family is implicated, causing Jo and Ben significant stress and expense, now Sean is shot, his family is turned upside down, and that poor woman who was killed has left six orphans and there are those Sloan children who are now parentless victims of circumstance as well … and we can't forget whoever did it. Hi family will, undoubtedly, be greatly affected as well."

"Well, now, that's British understatement for you," I thought to myself as I helped Galena with the dishes.

"From what I hear," Deirdre said, "those kids have been having problems for a long time. Ed never did much fathering, the drunken lout. It was Ginger who took care of them and now she's gone."

"They were picked up last night and will be placed in temporary foster care as soon as possible," Sean said. "Family Services doesn't like to keep young children in a facility for very long. It's better to get them into a home environment quickly."

"Wherever they are it will most likely be better than where they have been," I said." Then I turned to Galena, "Do you know what will happen to your friends children?"

"Oh, they be O.K. She have beeg family. They good people. They take good care of kids."

"How old are the children?" Deirdre asked.

"The big girl, she is fourteen, and the baby is three."

"Will they be able to keep all the children together?" I asked

"I don't think so. That is sad, but they all be here in Sonoma so they almost together."

"Well, that's something at least," Ross said as she folded the last dish towel.

"There," I said, putting away the last pot. "I think things are pretty much in hand now. I'd best be getting home."

"I'll be on my way as well," Ross said. "Would you like a ride back into town Galena?"

"I'll take her," I said. "I'm going right past her house." We all hugged Mrs. O'Malley, Deirdre and Sean. "You take care of yourself now Sean." We left the family to themselves.

Chapter 15

I had taken some brie, a baguette, grapes and a bottle of Ben's Zinfandel in a basket and gone to the Mountain cemetery in Sonoma to sit with old friends, relax and think.

O.K. O.K. So some of you may think a cemetery is a strange place to find relaxation and companionship. Me? I've always found old cemeteries very interesting and comforting too on occasion. Both at home and overseas, I find them fascinating and I enjoy the company I can keep. In cemeteries in the English countryside, I have picnicked with William Shakespeare in the Stratford on Avon cemetery and with Kenneth Graham and JRR Tolkien in Oxford. I have argued with Carl Marx in the Highgate Cemetery in London and I have lunched with Oscar Wild in the Père Lachaise Cemetery in Paris. Here at home I have taken a good book to Glenn Ellen and sat with Jack London while I read. Today I was planning on sharing my picnic with General Vallejo and the Haraszthys in the old Mountain Cemetery in Sonoma.

Although the case against Lee was growing weaker each day, the charges had not been dropped and until they were, I couldn't help but worry. The events at the O'Malleys had been unsettling to say the least. Those poor kids, loosing their mother, and so soon after their father was killed in a car crash. Father Sean had said that he and Deirdre would help them financially. That was great, however, it certainly couldn't replace parents.

On a slab of stone across from the Sebastiani tomb, I laid out my best heirloom paper towels to spread my picnic on, poured myself a glass of Zin in one of my very best heirloom plastic glasses, and with a fine plastic knife started to spread a bit of Brie on a chunk of baguette from the Basque Boulangerie. I sat looking out across the town and the hills beyond.

"Excuse me Ma'am..."

"I nearly jumped out of my skin. Whipping my head around, I saw a disreputable-looking figure standing behind me. He was tall and thin as a rail. His chin was covered with stubble and his eyes were watery and red-rimmed.

"Excuse me," he said again. "I sure could use a bit of that," and he indicated the bottle of wine. I'd be lying through my teeth if I said I wasn't damn near scared out of my pants; out here, alone and with this pretty scary looking individual. He sat down beside me and I instinctively glanced around for a weapon of some sort, but all I could see was the corkscrew and that puny plastic knife. Hell, there wasn't even a substantial rock near-to-hand. I soon realized however that I was in far greater danger of dying from exfoliation than I was of being attacked. The smell of this poor vagrant was staggering.

"I'm Harry," and his breath damn near knocked me over. He rubbed the stubble on his chin with the back of his hand and longingly eyed my bottle of Zin. I decided he couldn't be too dangerous; not if he sat down and told me his name; well, not dangerous if you discounted the eau d'vagrant.

"I'm Jo," I said. "May I offer you a glass of wine?" and I poured a bit into the extra plastic glass I had for no reason I could think of, brought with me. He hungrily grabbed it with both trembling hands and gulped down its contents. Some dribbled out the corners of his mouth and down his chin. I poured him a bit more and also spread some brie on a healthy chunk of baguette and handed it to him. He downed the second glass of wine and gobbled up the bread like he hadn't eaten in days, which, I would have been very willing to bet he hadn't. I gave him more bread and some of the grapes.

Watching him closely, though I had scooted away a bit in an attempt to avoid the his stench, I decided I had little to fear. He was filthy and pathetic but I didn't think he was at all dangerous.

"So Harry," I said after pouring him yet another glass of wine and giving him the rest of the bread and cheese, "What are you doing up here?"

"Well Mam,..."

"Jo," I corrected.

"Well Jo," he seemed uncomfortable using my first name, "Ma'am, I live here some of the time."

"Here in the cemetery?"

"Yes Ma'am, er...Jo. Right here. Just me and the ghosts."

"The ghosts?" I couldn't help laughing a bit.

"Yes Ma'am. Me and the ghosts; we're real good friends we are."

"So tell me about your ghost friends Harry."

"Oh we're good friends, me and the ghosts. We have some good ol' times, me and them."

"Doing what?"

"Oh, ... mostly they do the doing and I just sort of watch. Like a while back. It was raining and they was two of 'em. A man and a woman' and they was fightin'. I didn't know ghosts could fight, least ways not with each other. Did you know ghost could fight?"

"No I didn't," I smiled. "What were they fighting about?"

"Couldn't rightly hear much of what they was sayin', but they was sure goin' at it." He stopped, rubbed his chin again and stared at the nearly empty wine bottle. I poured the rest of the wine into his glass.

"Go on," I said. I knew it was just a little mean of me to lead him on but I was having a bit of fun listening to him. Besides, he might come up with something I could use in a book sometime. "Tell me more about your ghosts. Who won the fight?" I felt a little guilty about enjoying myself at his expense.

"Well, they was screaming at each other and he was drinking, and he threw the bottle away and then she jumped at him and scratched his face I think, least ways that's what it looked like, and then he hit her."

I leaned forward. This was something more than alcoholic ramblings or the DT's. "Go on," I encouraged. "Then what happened?"

94

"She fell down and he started yelling at her to get up but she wouldn't and he kept yelling at her and then it all just sort of went away."

"What do you mean, it all went away."

"Oh, it just went away. It always does. And there's never anything left in the morning."

"Harry, can you show me where your ghosts had their fight?"

"Sure can, Ma'am. It's right over there," and he pointed down the hill to the Vallejo tomb. We walked together down one of the lanes to the site of the ghostly battle.

I looked around but saw nothing out of the ordinary. Then I spotted something glittering out of the corner of my eye. There at the edge of the plot just below the Vallejo tomb was a bit of broken glass. I walked over to investigate and discovered what was obviously the remains of a broken beer bottle. It was partly covered with fallen leaves. Something told me not to touch it. I retraced my steps, treading as lightly as possible so as not to disturb any more of the surroundings than absolutely necessary. When we got back to where we had been sitting, I took out my cell phone and dialed.

"Hello, Allen? I'm in the old cemetery. I really think you should get up here as soon as possible. No, I'm not being funny, and no, I'm not drunk. You have to meet me here just as soon as possible. No! After work won't do! Now! You have to come now! No! Don't argue with me. Just get here. Please! There's someone here you really must talk to. Fifteen minutes? Fine. Yes, I can wait. I'll be by the Vallejo tomb. And Allen, you won't regret it, honest. " I snapped my phone shut and put it back in my pocket.

I had a hard time convincing Harry to stay and when Allen arrived it was even harder.

"So, what's all this 'ere then?" Allen said as he walked up a path towards us. He liked doing that. It was a bit of a joke with him. He'd found an old bobby's hat in an antique shop when he was on vacation in England two years ago. Ever since he'd loved to put on a pathetically poor attempt at an English accent and say things like, "'Ello, 'ello, 'ello," and "What's all this 'ere then," particularly around Ross which always caused her to grimace.

I introduced him to a rather reticent Harry, who, with the promise of a good meal and some cash found his tongue again. After interviewing Harry, I took Allen to where I'd seen the broken beer bottle. He briefly looked around and then called the department. Within half an hour the cemetery had been cordoned off and a forensic team was doing their thing with their proverbial fine-tooth combs and baggies.

As we watched, Allen received a call. When he disconnected he said something had come up and he had to go. He left and I took Harry into town and bought him his promised meal; fast food burgers by his choice. Knowing that the money Allen had given him would soon be converted into cheap wine, I arranged for Harry to have $50.00 worth of credit at the burger place and then went home, leaving him sitting at one of the outside tables working his way through three burgers, a double order of fries, a large soda and a berry turnover.

Chapter 16

The next morning's
headlines read like a tabloid:

Eye Witness Sez Ghost Killz Girl In Local Graveyard

The article, I am happy to say, was more
responsible, giving a fairly accurate account of
what had happened.   It went on to tell that
despite the rain and the elapsed time, the forensic
team had found tissue and hair on the edge of one of
the tomb stones. They had also made a cast of a tire
track left in the now dried mud just outside the gate at
the upper entrance to the cemetery. In addition to the
bits of broken glass from a beer bottle, they had found
fragments from a broken taillight.

Ben was reading the paper aloud at the breakfast table
when the phone rang. It was Allen.

"Just wanted to tell you Jo, that was some lead you gave us
yesterday. The tire casting matches one of the ones that was taken
at your place the morning the body was found. And the fragments of
tail light also match fragments we found at your place."

My heart sank. "Oh my God," I gasped.

"What are you fretting about?"

"That sounds like pretty damning evidence," I said, with my voice
near tears. Ben, Jay and Lee were staring at me.

"Oh Christ, Jo, don't you see? This pretty much gets Lee off the
hook.   The tread isn't from any of your vehicles, and, if you
remember, none of your vehicles had a broken tail light.   And none of

you own a red convertible."

"Red convertible? What does a red convertible have to do with anything?"

"This morning one of the Sloan kids told us that after Ginger came home that night she snuck out the bedroom window, walked down the road a little way, and got into a red convertible."

"Convertible? It was raining that night."

"One assumes, Jo, that the top was up. Anyway, I don't see how there can still be any charges against Lee or Alberto that will hold."

"Oh Allen," I said, and started to cry.

Jay snatched the phone from me. "What the hell did you say to my mother to make her cry? Aren't things bad enough without you ...oh...Wow! Hey! That's great!" He slammed the phone down, let out a war whoop and punched Lee in the shoulder. "Right on Bro,...'t's all fine. You're off the hook and so is Alberto! Lee leaned back in his chair, let out a long breath and said, "But, let's not crack the champagne until the charges are formally dropped."

"Ah, don't be such a pessimist, Bro."

"I just think it's best not to court trouble."

"I think Lee is right," I said. "It will all be O.K. soon enough."

"Well," Ben said, pushing back his finished plate, "Given this good news, there's no reason not to get a bit of work done today. Since this will all blow over soon, I assume you'll be going back to classes and I'll be loosing my two best workers."

"I don't know about Jay but I'm not going back until I know it's over for sure. I may just drop out all together. I can learn just as much about music playing it as I can at school. It's a waste of good money if you ask me."

Ben scowled at him over the rim of his glasses and I cleared my throat in preparation for my usual education speech.

"O.K. O.K." Lee said throwing up his hands. "It was just a thought. I'll meet you in the winery and he slipped out the door after snagging the last muffin.

I was at my desk looking out the window. I could see smoke on the east side of the valley. Must be some vintner burning off piles of vine prunings, I thought to myself. I was just returning to work when a car came roaring up the drive, its horn honking frantically. It showered gravel as it skidded to a stop. Alistair, George and Maggie of course added to the cacophony as they bolted from the winery to greet the arrival. Crap! And I was so hoping to get a bit of work done. I left my desk to go see who it was. When I peered out the kitchen window and saw Ross's M.G., I put the kettle on.

They didn't come in. Charley and Lacey extracted themselves from the M. G. Ross remained in the driver's seat and continued to blow the horn. I came out the kitchen door as Lee and Jay came running from the winery followed by Ben. The dogs were going ballistic with enthusiasm for this wonderful new game.

"What's wrong?" I shouted from the back stoop.

"What-the-hell's going on?" Ben yelled.

"They're going to arrest Rod Gardner for the murder," Charley shouted. "Hush! Listen!"

Ross's car radio picked up police, fire and ambulance calls. Just another of this "little old lady's" numerous hobbies. No wonder she didn't think she had time to write her memoirs.

"We were on our way over here when we heard it," she added. "We actually heard Allen say he was going to the Gardino's and that he wanted some backup."

"Good God!" I gasped.

"No!" Lee said. "Can't be! Rod's an asshole but he wouldn't kill someone. Anyway, I didn't think Allen was on the case anymore."

"Well, looks like he's back on," Charley said. "After all, he's about the best inspector they have."

"Couldn't happen to a nicer guy," Jay said.

"Shush," hissed Ross. "Perhaps we'll hear something more."

We all bent our ears to the car radio, but all we heard were squeaks and squawks of static. Then a call to rescue a dog who had fallen into an open drain pipe came through.

I heard the kettle shrilling and suggested that we all go into the kitchen.

Over coffee (Ross had tea) and yesterday's coffee cake, we speculated; letting our imaginations run wild.

"In high school he was a pompous asshole," Jay said, but I sure never would have pegged him for something like this."

"I wonder if the baby was his," I said as I poured more coffee.

"Most likely," Jay continued. "Getting into some girl's pants was always his major. If they gave scholarships for it, he would have gotten one for sure."

"It's my belief that all young men are pretty good at that," Lacey said, with a touch of frost.

"Now Dear, don't be a female chauvinist sow," Ross said, patting her on the hand.

"Hey," Jay said. "There's a big difference between a healthy libido and someone like Rod Gardino. When a guy is the focus of locker room talk, you know it's gotta be pretty bad. With him it wasn't like it was sex drive. It was like he was trying to prove something. There was a row of little gold stars pasted on his dash board. Said he didn't have a gun handle to carve notches on."

"How utterly revolting," Ross said with disgust.

"Don't you think you all may be jumping to conclusions," Ben said. "You only heard Allen say he was going to the Gardino's and for someone to meet him there. He didn't actually say he was going to arrest the kid.

We all looked at him silently for a moment. Then we had to admit that he was right. We were jumping to unfair conclusions.

Just then, the dogs began howling like timber wolves and in the distance we heard sirens. We looked at each other for a moment. "Take it easy," Ben said. It's just an ambulance or a fire truck. Might be because of the smoke."

"The smokes on the other side of the valley, Grump," Jay said. "That's a squad car, and it's heading down Arnold Road from the Gardino's." We all leapt from our chairs and raced out to Ross's M.G. and the car radio.

The reception wasn't clear, but we managed to make out that there were several squad cars giving chase to a red sports car. Periodically we could hear Allen's voice through the static. We were straining our ears to hear what was happening when we heard a chopper. The sheriff's department helicopter was gliding over the hills and along what we knew to be Arnold Drive. It appeared that the chase was heading towards Glenn Ellen.

On the car radio, we could hear the chopper giving directions to the forces on the ground. He was just passing the Sonoma Golf Club. We made out Allen's voice calling for more units to help cordon off the exits to Arnold Road. Unfortunately, there was an out-of-control fire in the dry hills on the east side of the valley. The chopper told Allen that it was going to take a while for help to arrive. Ross's radio was crackling with static, as the chase got further away however the string of Anglo Saxon expletives that Allen uttered came through loud and clear. "Shit!" he yelled. "We have to stop him before he gets into Glenn Ellen. The streets will be full of tourists. Someone'll get hurt. Get 'em here as fast as you can."

"They're on their way sir," the dispatcher answered. "It'll be about fifteen minutes."

"Christ! That'll be too late?"

"Sorry, Sir."

"There's no units closer?"

"You've already got 'em Sir."

"Swell."

The chase was approaching the Developmental Center. We could hear the chopper on his loudspeaker, warning the residents to keep clear of the road. Next, it passed the Olive Press. The chopper was flying low, hovering over the little red car and telling him to stop. Again, they warned him to stop. He was in Glenn Ellen now. "He just turned onto London Ranch Road," the chopper told the ground units.

"Stupid son-of-a-bitch!" Allen shouted. It's a dead end. Try to get in front and buzz him. There'll be tourists coming down from the ranch."

"Can't see him anymore, Sir. He's disappeared into a wooded part of the road; think I can get ahead of him just up the road a bit. There's a bit of open road about half a mile ahead, just before a bend."

"Good. You buzz him as he comes out of the trees and we'll cut him off from behind."

We could hear nothing but the chopper for a moment or two, then, "Oh Christ!" and there was silence. The next thing we heard was a call for an ambulance and fire truck and then everything went dead.

We looked at each other in silence. "I could use a belt," Ben said and headed for the house.

"If that's an offer," Ross said, "I accept. I could use something a bit more bolstering than tea myself."

We all trudged into the kitchen. Ben fetched his bottle of Irish and set it on the table. Lee, Charley and I opted for a bottle of Anchor Steam instead.

"The hell of it is," I said, "I can't call Allen to find out what's happening because he's there."

"It's time for the local news," Lee said. "They might have something." We all trooped into the den and huddled around the tube as Ben tuned in the local channel.

"...and this story just breaking," said the pretty, young anchor. "A high speed chase of a suspect in the Ginger Sloan murder case has just ended in a potentially fatal crash. We now go to Greg Hanson on location."

"Thank you Miranda. This is Greg Hanson, on location on London Ranch Road, just outside of Glenn Ellen, where a red convertible driven by a young man wanted for questioning in the Ginger Sloan murder case has just skidded out of control and collided with an oncoming truck carrying a load of grapes. The convertible burst into flames moments after the driver was removed. He's being taken to Community Hospital and is reported to be in critical condition. The driver of the truck is being treated for minor cuts and bruises. As you can see, the road is blocked with the wreckage of the convertible and the overturned bens of grapes the truck was carrying. These were probably Zinfandel grapes from the estate vineyards on Jack London Ranch. Emergency crews are on their way to clear the road. This is a two-lane road, dead-ending at Jack London Historical State Park which is a high tourist destination aria. Officers are directing cars to turn and go back to the park. Park rangers are helping to direct traffic at their end and keep visitors as calm as possible until the road is cleared. Back to you Mira... no...wait...there appears to be a new development...something's going on about half a mile back up the line of stranded vehicles." The reporter's mike went dead for a moment and we could see him talking to Allen. In the distance, we could see the chopper settling down beside the road and a flurry of activity. "Yes, ladies and gentlemen...we do have a new development. A woman in one of the stranded vehicles has gone into premature labor. Since authorities have no idea how long it will take to clear the road the helicopter is going to airlift her to the hospital. Park rangers are helping her into the chopper. Now, back to you Miranda.

"Thank you Greg. And this just in. The injured driver of the convertible is Rod Gardino, Jr. Police went to the Gardino home late this morning to arrest Gardino, Jr. on suspicion of murder in the Ginger Sloan case. As police arrived Rod Gardino, Jr. jumped into his car and lead authorities on a high-speed chase that eventually involved three Sonoma Police and Sonoma county Sheriffs' units, plus the sheriff department's helicopter. The chase, ended as you have just seen when Gardino, Jr's. vehicle went out of control and collided with a winery truck, carrying a load of Zinfandel grapes from vineyards at the Jack London estate. We'll keep you updated as we receive new information."

"And, get this ladies and gentlemen; police said they went to the Gardino home as the result of a tip given them by ghosts in the old Mountain Cemetery. So, Bob," she said turning to her co-anchor, "do you think this is the latest thing in crime detection?"

"Sounds to me like there's some fun and games going on at the police station," the co-anchor said as he mimed taking a drag off a joint. "And on the sports scene today; the city of San Francisco and the Niners are still locked in debate over..."

Ben snapped the set off with disgust. "Assholes," he muttered.

Chapter 17

Allen called in the late afternoon and asked if it would be O.K. if he dropped by after work.

"Of course," I said. "Come and have dinner with us. I'm making pot roast."

"And let me guess, it just happens to be made with Zinfandel, right?"

"You got it."

"Sounds great Jo. I'd love to, but I have no idea when it'll be, Jo. I have to file my reports before I can leave and I'm not even back at the office yet. We're still at the scene of the accident. Better not wait dinner on me."

"O.K. We won't, but I'll have something for you whenever you show up."

"Thanks Jo. I appreciate it. I just really need a good friend for a while this evening. See you tonight. Perhaps we can go have a drink someplace quiet."

"That would be nice Allen. I could use some quiet time with a good friend myself."

Having overheard my conversation, Jay leaned in at my office door. "So, things getting hot and heavy between you and Allen?"

"Of course not. He just wants some company with a good friend this evening, that's all."

"Yea, right Ma. He has dozens of good friends. If company with a friend's all he wants, why call you? Most guys would go out for a beer with another guy. Face it Ma. He's got the hots for you."

"Damn it! He does not and stop calling me Ma." Jay flashed me his big grin, shrugged his shoulders and sauntered down the hall with his hands in his pockets whistling "Love Is in the Air."

We had an early dinner and I spent the rest of the evening at my desk.

Allen arrived about eight thirty. I heated up some of the pot roast, which incidentally had turned out exceptionally well. I really recommend marinating your meat in Zinfandel, and a lot of garlic, the next time you do a pot roast. I also made a small fresh salad. Ben was in his office working on his books. Jay and Lee had gone to their rooms to read. They said they had a lot of catching up to do what with all the classes they had missed, however it was early enough in the semester that they were both considering withdrawing from classes and starting fresh in the spring. When they had mentioned this to Ben he had blown a gasket, so they said they guessed they had better start studying.

It was a warm and beautiful evening so when Allen had finished his supper we decided not to go out, but instead took a bottle of Ben's Zinfandel to the veranda, which overlooked the pond. When the farm had first been built, the pond was necessary for irrigation. Ben had dug new, deeper and better wells to irrigate the vineyards, so the ponds main function now was as a home for ducks. There was a small wooden pier to which a dilapidated rowboat was moored. When they were little, the boys would fish from it and on occasion, catch the unwary stickleback or bluegill.

"Jesus what a day," Allen said as he poured the wine. I leaned back in a wicker chaise and lit a cigarette.

"I didn't know you smoked, Jo."

"I don't. I quit 15 years ago when we moved in with Ben. He won't allow smoking in the house so it seemed like a good time to quit. This is a temporary relapse...what with all the crap that's been going on. Dumb, I know."

"It's your lungs," he said with a shrug.

We sat quietly for a while drinking our wine and listening to the evening sounds: the ducks and other bird life settling in for the night, Cindy and the goats munching a last snack before sleep. Marmalade and Fritz had accompanied us to the veranda. Marmalade lay curled in my lap, running his motor and kneading biscuits, while Fritz wandered out to stalk through the rushes at the edge of the pond, in hopes of finding some unwary wee creature not yet bedded down for the night. We watched the final light fade from the sky and the moon rise over the Sonoma mountains.

"It's certainly easy to see why the local Indians called it 'The Valley of the Moon'," Allen said, taking a sip of his wine.

"Yes indeed," I answered dreamily. Then I sat up suddenly, startling Marmalade off my lap. "So, Allen, just what the hell happened today? Why did you go to the Gardino's? The news said you went there to arrest Rod Jr."

"Well, not exactly. As usual, the media got things a little mixed up. We only wanted to talk to him. A lot of things led in that direction, but we certainly didn't have enough at that time to make an arrest."

"So, what did make you go there, if I may ask?"

"O.K.," he said, taking another sip of wine. "I think I already told you that the tail light material and the imprint of the tire we found at the cemetery matched what we found here, and they both came from a classic Corvette. Then when the Sloan kid said he saw Ginger climb out the window and meet someone in a red convertible, things started to click. We knew Rod Jr. had a red convertible classic Corvette. Hell, he's been stopped for speeding often enough. Just how many bright red vintage Corvettes do you think there are in Sonoma County?"

"When we drove out to the Gardino place, Rod, Sr. blustered and said we couldn't come in and to get the hell off his property or he'd make things damn hot for us. We could see Rod, Jr. in the entryway behind his father, pacing up and down. He looked like he was about to jump out of his skin. Rod, Sr. told him to stay calm. He had nothing to worry about. He said I was only there to divert attention from Lee because you and I were going together. Then Jr. disappeared. "

"I assume," I said, "that 'going together,' aren't the exact words he used."

Allen blushed and cleared his throat before going on. "He said there wasn't a damn thing I could do and I knew it. However when I produced a search warrant he changed his tune. He went from blustering to being sickeningly sweet, however he continued to make references to your and my relationship."

"I didn't know we had a relationship; well, beyond good friends that is."

Allen looked just a wee bit hurt as he continued. "Rod, Sr. grabbed the warrant and was reading it when Jr. appeared in the driveway; apparently he had gone out the back, he leapt into his car and took off like the proverbial bat-out-of- hell. You pretty much know the rest."

"Is he going to be O.K.?"

"They won't know for a while. He was pretty badly broken up. They said he'll be in intensive care for quite a while. There's an officer at the hospital, over his father's protests. It's not like he could go anywhere, but it's regulations."

"What's going to happen to him? Running like that rather amounts to a confession, doesn't it?"

"That, of course, is up to the D. A. He may feel it amounts to a confession, yet again, he may figure he just panicked. I don't think the D. A. or any judge in this county is going to be likely to cut any member of the Gardino family much slack. They haven't exactly gone out of their way to make friends since they moved here. First, however, the kid has to get well enough to stand trial. He'll probably be pretty badly crippled up for quite awhile. It's more than just broken bones. The last report we had said that one lung was punctured and that he has a broken spleen. Fortunately, for him, his father is wealthy enough to hire the best medical care available. Also, the best attorneys."

"I should think that the evidence of his car being at both locations would be pretty damming."

"To be absolutely fair, at this point we don't know for sure that it was his car; just that it was a vintage red Corvette, but like I said before, his is about the only one around. The final lab analyses should be back quite soon however. Even then, it'll have to be proved that he was driving it. His attorney will of course say that the car was stolen."

"And the theft went unreported?"

"Exactly. In my book, the evidence is pretty damning, but who knows what a clever attorney can do?"

"He's a known womanizer."

"That's not against the law."

"She was underage and she was pregnant."

"Now, Jo. We don't know if it was his yet. I know he wasn't very likeable but he is entitled to a fair trial."

"Yah, right. As fair as the way his father has managed to get his hands on half the county. Gawd-damn vulture."

"Being a prick doesn't necessarily make him guilty, Jo."

"Oh, I know. Damn, I'm glad I've never been called to sit on a jury. I'd have a hard time being totally objective. Anyway, this means all charges against Lee and Alberto will be dropped, doesn't it?"

"I would be irresponsible if I said yes, however, off the record, I think you can breathe easy now."

"When do you think they will charge him; Rod, that is?"

"That will depend on his medical condition. His dad can afford the best attorneys and you can bet they will be in on it from the get-go. I would assume they will try to forestall his being charged as long as possible."

"What about Ed Sloan? What's going to happen there? After all, there were dozens of witnesses in his case."

"I should think it's pretty much an open-and-shut case. He'll probably have a public defender. Don't think there's any way he can afford a private attorney. I think his only defense might be mental anguish over the loss of his daughter. Of course, his previous behavior and lack of concern for his kids isn't going to help him with that line of defense."

Just then, Jay stuck his head out his bedroom window and called down to us, "Hey, it's a beautiful night. You two taking advantage of it?" I could have gleefully strangled him.

"Mind your business," I shouted up at him.

"Just asking. Jeeses! Don't be so touchy Ma."

"Don' call me Ma!.

"O.K., O.K." He threw his hands up, withdrew back into his room. I heard him mutter, "Just trying to help things along." I was thoroughly embarrassed and I was sure Allen was as well.

He gracefully altered the situation by saying, "Oh, incidentally, the woman who was air-lifted to hospital; she was safely delivered of a nine pound boy. She named him London. Well Jo, it's getting late," he added, "and I have to be back on duty early. Thanks for supper and the company. I really needed to be with someone this evening."

"So did I Allen. It was nice. Thanks." We held hands as we walked around the house to the back where his car was parked. Before getting in the car he kissed me. Not a passionate kiss; I'd call it a companionable kiss. Nonetheless, it did make me wonder if the boys were right.

Chapter 18

Sean still couldn't drive and since Deirdre was so busy at the winery, Ross had volunteered to act as chauffeur. Father Sean's was a small and traditional parish and he performed the duties of a traditional cleric. He visited those of his flock who were in the hospital or shut-ins at home. He visited young mothers who had just delivered and he visited those who had just lost a loved one. Today he had brought two lonely hearts together. An elderly gentleman dying of cancer had lost his aged canine companion of nearly a quarter of a century. Father Sean had heard of an old mostly Labrador at the local animal control who was about to be put down. It's always difficult to find homes for old dogs. Sean brought the two together and it was love at first site.

After finishing their rounds, they had dropped by in hopes of finding a cup of tea or a glass of wine and a bit of conversation.

"I've written my sermons for the next two months, rewritten my wedding service, and managed to beat the top level of my computer's chess game. With Deidre and my mother too busy this time of year, I'm dying for good conversation, or at least a bit of gossip."

"How's the leg coming?" I asked.

"A lot better since they removed the drain yesterday. The doctors said it's doing well but they still have forbidden me to drive for at least two weeks. In the meantime Ross has been pressed into service."

"And loving every moment of it," she said, sipping her tea. "I had no idea just what a priest did besides offer people wine and wafers. And," she continued enthusiastically, "I'm going to be helping him with the research for his book."

"What book?" I asked.

"Oh, the one I've been working on for the past 15 years."

"Oh that one." I laughed.

"You can laugh now but you just wait till it comes out and the truth be known about all your ancestors. There's a lot of skeletons rattling around in Sonoma County closets."

"I still think you ought to turn it into a novel about your family," I said.

"Perhaps I don't want people to know that my great grandfather was a gambler with a price on his head. Might not look too good for a priest to have a murderer for an ancestor you know," he chuckled.

"Not a murderer, a patriot," I said.

Ross pursed her lips. "Hmm. Might have been one of my ancestors he killed."

Sean's great-grandfather, old Sean Gavin O'Malley, had fled Ireland with a price on his head after the mysterious bombing of an English army barracks in which two English soldiers had been killed.

"Sure-an tats, true me Pet," he answered in mock a brogue. "If any of your ancestors had been part of the odious army of occupation..."

"Hush!" I hissed. "For Christsake, let's not set Ben off. I'm not up for a tirade at the moment." Just then, the phone rang. It was Allen.

"Hi, Jo. I'm just about to finish up here. Thought I'd drop by if I may. I have some news you'll be glad to hear."

"Wonderful Allen. Sean and Ross are here."

"Good. They'll be interested too."

About half an hour later Alistair, George and Maggie announced Allen's arrival. They worked themselves into a frenzy of excitement whenever Allen arrived. In the line of duty, he often found himself entering property where the canine population was not nearly as genial as Ben's pack. Stuffing his pockets with doggie treats usually forestalled what might otherwise be an unpleasant altercation. Once he was foolish enough to make Alistair, George and Maggie aware of this great benefice. They now expected a handout every time he arrived. Alistair and George had to wait until the treats were offered. Maggie however was tall enough that she merely put her nose in his pocket and helped herself.

"O.K. O.K. he laughed. "Enough now!" He bent to give each a perfunctory pat on the head before coming into the kitchen and pouring himself a cup of coffee. He pulled up a chair and sat; a row of salivating faces waiting hopefully for an additional handout. "That's all," he said to them. "You've cleaned me out." Alistair let out a little woof and wriggled his butt. George lay down with his nose between his paws and looked up at Allen in what he hoped was a seductive manner. Maggie just stuck her huge nose in his pocket.

"Cheeky buggers," Ross said with a laugh.

"Yes Alan," I added. I'm afraid you've created quite a monster."

"Three, actually. Look!" He said turning his pockets inside out. "All gone!" Alistair, being a fair weather friend got up and trotted off, soon to be followed by George who stopped at the door and gave a last hopeful look over his shoulder. Maggie however, being made of sterner stuff continued to sit with one huge paw on Allen's knee gazing imploringly into his face, ropes of saliva decorating his trousers.

"That's enough Maggie! Out!" I shouted. She gave several little annoyed puffs and then slowly retreated to the door where she stood and gave Allen an imploring last look before slowly making her exit. "You don't have to put up with that Allen, but it serves you right for having started it in the first place. "

He went to the sink and using a soiled dishtowel, tried to wipe the dog drool off his pant leg. "This stuff's adhesive," he said as he washed his hands. "You should try marketing it. How's the leg coming along Father Sean?"

"Ah, it's a damn bother, but it seems to be healing O.K. Can't drive yet though so Ross has benevolently offered chauffer services. Getting in and out of that sardine can she calls a car with this gimpy leg however is a bit like being taken with instruments," he laughed.

"Well I like that!" Ross exclaimed.

"You said you had news, Allen. What's up?" I asked.

"Rod Gardino confessed to the killing this morning. He made a full statement."

"So, he's out of hospital then?" Ross asked.

"No, he's still in the hospital but he's out of ICU and doing as well as can be expected. He called us. Said he wanted to tell us what happened. His father and his attorney were both present. According to him, he had done a lot of crank that night. Turns out he'd been using since high school."

"Good heavens!" exclaimed Ross.

"Too much money and too much free time," I grumbled.

Allen continued, "He said that he had been drinking that night as well."

"Bad combination," I added.

"After he dropped Ginger off he drove Alberto home and then drove to a liquor store, bought several quarts of beer and just drove around drinking. Ginger called him on his cell phone and said she had to see him. Said she would sneak out her window and meet him at the end of the road. Evidently, they had been having an on-again, off-again affair for quite some time but he planned to tell her that night that it was over. After all, he was getting married to the Leventhal girl in a month."

"Poor girl," I said.

"He said he didn't think it would bother her," Allen continued, "because she played around so much. The old cemetery was a place they used to meet so he took her there to tell her."

"In the rain? That's pretty strange," I said.

Allen shrugged his shoulders and continued. "He said when he told her she became hysterical and said he had to marry her because she was pregnant. He claimed it couldn't have been his kid."

"How could he be sure it wasn't?" I asked, "Particularly if he was using drugs. He probably didn't always think to use any protection."

"Well, tests will show if it was his or not. Anyway, he claims killing her was an accident. Said they were arguing; he called her a slut, said she slept around so much it could be half the counties kid.

She flew at him and clawed his face."

"She was good at that." Lee said. He had just come into the kitchen to make himself a sandwich and overheard the last part of Allen's narrative. He went to the fridge. "O.K. if I use some of this meat loaf Ma."

"If you quit calling me Ma."

"O.K., Mom.

"Go ahead Allen," I said.

"So, when she clawed him he back-handed her and she fell. He thinks she must have slipped and hit her head. He thought she was just fooling around, trying to get sympathy. He shouted at her; kept telling her to get up. When he realized she was dead he panicked; carried her up to the old back gate of the cemetery, managed to get her over the wall and then brought his car around. Said he drove around for a long time drinking beer and trying to figure out what to do."

"Jesus," I said. "If he'd gone straight to the police and told them it was an accident..."

"Remember Jo, he was high and drunk and not thinking too straight. Anyway, he said he has no idea why he drove up here to your place. He's not even sure he remembers doing it, but when he got here and saw the bins of grapes he got Ginger out of the trunk of his car, put her in one of them, piled grapes over her and left.

"How utterly disgusting," Ross said.

"Poor lad," Sean said, "He must have been in constant turmoil ever since."

"Poor Ginger," Lee mumbled. He was leaning against the counter eating his sandwich as he listened to the conversation.

"But why did he run when you came to his home?" I asked.

"The crank, Mom." Lee said. That shit fryers your brain, particularly if you didn't have much of one to begin with."

"Oh don't be facetious," I snapped. "So, Allen, what do you think will happen to him? Is it murder or an accident?"

"Who knows? His dad has hired an army of attorneys and detectives. If tests show that the fetus wasn't his it will definitely better his chances.

"Well it looks like it's all over now," Lee said.

"Something like this is never really over is it," Sean said sadly.

"How so?" Lee asked.

"No matter what the legal outcome the negative impact is far reaching and long-lasting. He smiled at the quizzical look on Lee's face. "You think not? Let's start with you. You may be totally exonerated buy you've been in jail now. That has affected you and it can't be taken back, to say nothing of the financial impact it has had on your family."

"The money's nothing," Ben said. He had just come in. "Just so long as Lee's safe now."

"And there's the impact on Alberto's family. Just look at the trauma Mrs. Mendez has gone through, and the pay Alberto lost while he was in jail. What about that poor woman who was killed at our house, and her family. That can never be repaired. Even me. The doctor says I may have a limp for the rest of my life. And then there's the poor Sloan children. No Ginger to take care of them and now no father. They will be in foster care from now on.

"From what I hear," I said, "that may be an improvement."

"Well, be that as it may ... it is still all part of the domino effect of such an event."

"And we can't forget the effect on Rod himself," Allen added. "Even if his dad's fancy attorneys were to get him off scot free, the doctors say it is possible he will never be out of a wheelchair again. And of course there's Ed Sloan."

"Yes, what about him?" Ross asked.

"Oh, undoubtedly he's guilty." Allen answered. "After all there were several dozen witnesses to his act. His only defense will be temporary insanity due to bereavement."

"What's going to happen to the Sloan children?" Ross asked.

"They are in temporary foster care," Sean said. "Ironically they are staying with a family who have a small vineyard."

"Why is that ironic?" Ben asked."

"Don't you remember how Ed Sloan hates 'all you rich wine bastards'?"

"Oh right."

"How are they doing," Ross asked.

"The youngest boy seems to be doing well. The family keeps quite a few animals and he loves them. We are however, quite concerned about the girl and the oldest boy."

"How so?" I asked.

"The boy is incredibly angry. Angry at himself and everyone else except his sibling; and he won't let anyone else touch either of them, particularly the little girl."

"He's probably just appointed himself their protector now that Ginger's gone," I said. "I understand it was Ginger who took care of the little ones after the mother left.

"Most likely. The little girl is virtually catatonic. She almost never speaks and she hides all the time.

"Hides?" Lee asked, "like in hide and seek?"

No, like in hiding from life. They find her in the back of closets, under beds behind the sofa, in cabinets. It's an old Victorian house with an old flower bin in the pantry. They found her in there once. Fortunately, they don't keep flour in it any more. One time she hid in a big burlap sack of potatoes."

"Weird," Lee said.

"I guess I'd hide from life too if my mother had deserted me, my sister had been killed and my father was a murderer," Ross said. "What will happen to the poor little creatures?" she continued. "Will they be placed in permanent foster care?"

"I would certainly assume so," Father Sean said.

"I think the authorities have to make all efforts to try and find any family members," Allen said, "including the absent mother. And, as inappropriate as it seems, a lot will depend on the outcome of the father's trial. Even in jail he has some rights to his kids."

"That's absolutely appalling!" Ross spat. "Utterly despicable.!"

"Yep," Allen said as he rose. "There's a lot about the law that doesn't seem quite fair. Well, I have to be on my way. Just wanted to bring you up to date. Both Lee and Alberto can rest easy now. I should think all charges will be officially dropped in the morning."

"Thanks Allen." I rose to walk to the door with him. "I really appreciate your taking the time out to come by."

"Hey, me too," Lee called after him.

"I'll call you in a day or two. Remember, we still have a dinner date, and he gave me a friendly peck on the cheek."

"That would be nice Allen," I said.

"Dinner! Great idea," Ben said. "We have to have a dinner to celebrate the end of this business. I still say the only reason my Lad was implicated was political revenge ... couldn't get at me any other way ..."

"Yea Ben, sure," Allen said as he ducked out the door. He turned and called to me, "I'll call about dinner Jo." He walked down the path to his car with a hopeful canine escort. I stood at the screen door and watched him drive away. "Perhaps life will get back to normal now," I muised to myself.

Chapter 19

Well, so it had started out as a small dinner for family and a few close friends to celebrate the charges against Lee being officially dropped. Do there were the four of us, and of course we couldn't think of not inviting Allen, father Sean, Ross and Charley; that made eight, still a reasonable size for a dinner party, a and we could all fit around the dining table. Lacey had by this time become quite close with the family, so we decided to invite her as well. That made nine, which didn't fir around the table quite so nicely, so we decided to make it buffet instead of sit-down.

And since Alberto had been in it with Lee, and had also been totally exonerated, of course we invited him, which meant we also invited his mother and younger sibling. Sean said how glad his mother and Deidre were that things had worked out so well and we realized we couldn't leave them out. Deidre asked if she could bring the gentleman she was currently seeing. Of course she could and now the event was moved from the house to the veranda, which could accommodate more people.

Lee and Jay informed me nonchalantly that they had each invited "a few" friends, as had Alberto. So now our intimate family dinner had become a major event and it was moved from the veranda to the meadow between the winery and the pond, where the large BBQ pit was. Instead of the few appetizers, hand-made ravioli in fresh tomato-basil sauce and salad I had originally planned on serving, it was decided to butcher a pig, no, better make it two pigs, and a couple of dozen chickens. The boys thought it would be nice if Ross gave me her recipe for Cornish pasties. She benevolently said she would bring some and Alberto's mother said she'd bring tamales. The kids also thought potato salad, blackberry cobbler, and hand-cranked ice-cream would round things off nicely.

I was in the kitchen making the shopping list and organizing the logistics and wondering who I could hire to help me. I know Charley and Ross would help, but I wanted them to relax and have a good time. "Hell," I said, throwing down my pen. I want to have a good time too." I tore up my shopping list, went to the back door and yelled out to the pig pen that they were safe for a while. We weren't going to have BBQ'd piggy.

I poured myself a glass of ice tea, sat back down at the kitchen table with a fresh tab let and began making a new menu. "Do-it-yourself Kebabs," I said. All I have to do is dice the meat and vegetables. People will have a great time choosing their own items and grilling their own skewers. We'll have roasted corn, and let's see..." as I was musing on what else to have, I heard on the news that the Sonoma County crab season was opening early this year. "That's it!" I cried. "Crabs and oysters. We can boil the crabs outside on the BBQ and we'll BBQ the oysters. My kitchen will stay mostly clean and the boys and Ben will do most of the cooking. Besides, all men feel they know more about BBQ-ing than any woman ever born." I poured another glass of ice tea and wrote up my menu and shopping list. I was quite pleased with myself. For dessert I added watermelon.

*   *   *

The party was a rousing success and I, oh clever girl that I am, was able to enjoy it as much as everyone else. The two kegs of Anchor Steam and the several cases of Ben's wind had certainly helped things along. Although Ben is known for his old growth Zinfandel, he does make other excellent wines as well so, besides the Zin, he supplied a lovely Chenin Blanc to accompany the crabs and oysters.

It seemed like half the county showed up to help us celebrate, most bearing a contribution to the groaning board and congratulations for Lee and Alberto. Though these contributions had been neither solicited nor expected, they were greatly appreciated, including Lacey's bean salad which somehow managed to have gotten knocked off the table. George, Maggie and Alistair enjoyed it very much.

And I would be lying if I said that my guys remained strictly sober, but hell, after the stress they'd been under I couldn't blame them. Alberto and Lee seemed to be in competition with each other for most inebriate status of the evening, for which poor Alberto paid a high price when his mother saw him. One didn't have to have a scholarly command of the Spanish language to understand exactly what she was saying when she leaned him against the trunk of a tree and shook him back and forth by the shoulders. Alberto simply grinned foolishly, his head lolling from side to side as he sheepishly answered, "Si, Madré, si."

I was a bit more sympathetic with Lee and Jay's condition, partly because I knew their grandfather would cut them no slack the following morning, no matter how big their heads or fragile their stomachs. As the party ended, the last I saw of poor Alberto was his mother shoveling him into the back of their old pick-up among the gardening tools and burlap sacks, before herself climbing behind the wheel and rattling off down the drive, leaving a trail of Spanish expletives behind her.

The affair met with everyone's (except Alberto's mother's) approval. Only one person fell into the duck pond and amazingly, it wasn't one of the young inebriates. Despite the fact that I had told her it was a casual affair, Lacey had come dressed to the teeth and wearing stiletto-spiked heels. She was standing on the old wooden dock with a glass of wine in one hand and a plate of cracked crab in the other, trying to figure out just how to eat it when she caught one of her heels in a knothole and over she went, designer suit, crab, wine and all. Alberto and Lee fished her out, not an easy task given their state of intoxicating. Ross and Charley bundled her off to my room, dried her off and dressed her in one of my old muu-muus and a pair of sandals. Terribly embarrassed at first, she soon relaxed with the help of more Chenin Blanc and later admitted that she began having much more fun after her dunking than before. I think there's hope for the gal yet.

I had been right. Next morning Ben, with what I am sure was a bit of malicious glee, rousted the guys out of bed bright and early, throbbing heads, fragile stomachs and all. The day had dawned right and hot, which did not help their condition, for by the time they started the cleanup it had rendered the scattered crab and oyster shells quite odiferous. Lee lost the breakfast he hadn't had into the duck pond and Jay said he had two heads, both of them twice normal size and banging against each other. I swear Ben was enjoying himself tremendously.

Things were nearly back to normal by mid-afternoon. Ben and the boys had buried all the shells, corn cobs and watermelon rinds at the back of the garden where they would become more rich earth in a year. The trestle tables were stored back in the barn and BBQ pit was cleaned. I had the kitchen back to normal; all the leftovers were stored and the dishes washed. Alister, George and Maggie had gone with Ben to return the two empty beer kegs and the cats, who feigned total exhaustion, were stretched out on the veranda with Lee and Jay. "Now," I thought to myself, "that is an end to all this and I can perhaps concentrate on finishing that damn book."

Chapter 20

It was about a week after the party. I was in the kitchen working on the last of the recipes for the book when the phone rang. "You gonna be home for a bit Jo?" It was Allen. "I have some news I want to tell you before it hits the media."

"Sure. I'm working on the last of the recipes for the book, which fortunately is damn near finished."

"O.K. I'll be there in a few minutes. Can't talk you out of a bit of lunch, can I?"

"Absolutely. I'll use you as a guinea-pig."

"Oh darn," he laughed. "That'll be hard to take," and he hung up.

I went back to work. Like I had told Allen, I was working on the last of the recipes, Cornish Game Hens in a Zinfandel glaze and figs poached in Zinfandel.

I was just putting finishing touches on the game hens when Allen arrived. He had Father Sean with him. They both looked less than jubilant.

"I hope you don't mind my inviting myself along," Father Sean said as he gave me a kiss on the cheek. I know it's crass to crash a luncheon engagement."

'You know you're always welcome here Sean, but why the long faces? You both look like gravediggers. It's a beautiful day. What's wrong?" I poured them each a tall glass of minted ice tea, then sat down. "O.K. Come on. Out with it. What's up? What has you both so down in the dumps?"

Allen took a swallow of his tea. "Today is one of the few days when I wish I hadn't gone into police work. I hate knowing that this sort of thing can happen."

"For Christ sake Allen! Quit beating around the bush. What the hell has happened?"

"We wanted to come tell you before you heard it on the news," Father Sean said.

"Before what hit the news? Tell me!" I almost screamed.

"The lab report came back today," Allen said. "Rod Gardino wasn't the father of Ginger's baby."

My hand flew to my throat. "Oh my God," I gasped as adrenalin surged through my body. My first thought was that this meant it was Lee's. Why else would Allen and Father Sean want to tell me before I heard it on the news? I was numb. Sean reached out and took my hand. I jerked it away, jumped up and began pacing. "Oh my God," I said again.

"Calm down Jo," he said. "It's not what you're thinking."

"No," Allen said. "The DNA tests show that Ginger's unborn baby was fathered by, Ed Sloan, her own father."

"Oh surely not," I gasped as I sank back down in my chair; simultaneously relieved and repulsed. "There has to be some mistake."

"No. There's no mistake," Allen said.

"Oh that poor kid. No wonder she was so messed up. They say that sort of thing destroys a person."

"And there's more, Sean said. "it gets worse."

"How could it get any worse?" I asked. Then I conjured up the image of a little girl hiding in a sack of potatoes. "Oh no. Not the little one too?"

Sean nodded his head. "I'm afraid so."

"How did you find out?"

"When the lab report came in I was stunned," Allen said. Then I remembered the temporary foster parents telling about how the little girl hid all the time and how the older boy wouldn't let anyone touch the two little ones." I asked Sean to come with me and we drove out to the Murdock's place to talk to the kids. It took quite a bit of coaxing but once the older boy, Jimmy, opened up he couldn't be stopped. He told us how he would hear his father at night with Ginger; that the father told Ginger if she told anyone they would say she was crazy and lock her up because no one would believe a kid. Then he told her if she wasn't there for him he would just have to use Betsy, the little girl or even little Jack. So, ginger let him do it so he would leave the little ones alone. However, the boy said he knew his father had molested his youngest sister sometimes too."

"We asked him why he hadn't told anyone," Sean added, "and he told us he was scared to death of his dad; they all were. He kept loaded guns in the house and they were afraid he would use them. They thought of running away but they were afraid he would find them wherever they went."

"Jimmy, that's the older boy's name, told us that when the father was gone on a drinking spree Ginger would sing to them and tell them stories. She told them she was going to marry a very rich man and that she and her husband would adopt them all and take them away and they would all live together on a farm and each one would have a pony of their own and be able to eat strawberry shortcake every day. She had had strawberry shortcake once and told them how good it was."

"That monster," I said, almost to myself. "And oh, poor, poor little Ginger. No wonder she threw herself at guys, particularly Rod Gardino. I guess he was the wealthiest guy she knew. And the poor little ones. What is going to happen to them now?"

"The Murdocks would like to adopt them permanently, but it's a long tedious process. In the meantime they will be left with them in temporary foster care," Sean said. "I think the chances of the adoption going through are quite good. The Murdocks are a good and loving family. They are in good shape financially. They have been members of my flock for years. I doubt if there will be any trouble. It's just an incredible amount of red tape. The youngest boy loves it there. He seems to be the least affected of the three. They will all be going into intensive therapy as soon as possible.

"The Murdocks have already signed Jimmy up for classes at the local school. He should be entering fourth grade. He will most likely be behind since he has missed so much school. Betsy isn't old enough to enter school yet and although Jack should be in first grade, Mrs. Murdock feels Betsy will be better off if Jack is at home with her, at least for a while. Their case worker agrees with her."

"What a damn mess," I said. "Those poor kids. The son of a bitch ought to have his balls cut off."

"I totally agree with you Jo," Allen said.

"Have you heard what's happening with Rod?" I asked.

"With this new development I have a feeling the most he will get is man slaughter."

"I don't understand how Ed Sloan's behavior can alter the fact that Rod killed that poor girl and stuffed her in a bin of our grapes."

"I don't think his case will ever go to trial," Allen said. "I'm sure his battery of attorneys will be able to achieve a plea bargain."

"Besides," Sean added. "The latest word from the hospital is that it's very likely he will get a life sentence to a wheel chair. It turns out that there is such massive nerve damage it's unlikely he'll ever regain the use of his legs."

"And of course his father is bringing suit against the police and sheriffs' departments," Allen added.

"Do you think he'll win?" I asked.

"Not much, but you never know."

"Well," I sighed. "I guess that pretty much wraps things up. Will you open this Sean? I said, handing him a bottle of Ben's Zin as I began serving lunch.

Epilogue

It had been six months since the morning Ginger Sloan's body had been found in Ben's old-growth Zinfandel grapes. Things were pretty much back to normal. The Zinfandel cookbook was selling moderately well. Ben's Zinfandel had won two gold medals at the harvest festival and Lee had won the San Francisco Symphony's young musician award. Ben was more proud of that than of all the gold his Zins had ever received.

Ed Sloan had received life in prison without possibility of parole and yes, Rod Gardino Jr. had indeed received a sentence of life in his wheelchair. As much as I disliked him, that was still a harsh sentence for one so young.

Allen and I finally did manage our dinner date, and we went out a few times after that as well, but despite what good friends we were, or perhaps because of it, things just didn't click. I had assumed that he'd wind up with Charley. I knew she was quite smitten with him, however, surprise, surprise, he started dating Lacey and they were now quite a number. We all remained very good friends. There was a wine rep that I dated now and then and I'd gone out a few times with the food editor of the local newspaper. My boys were far more concerned about my love life than I was. They kept trying to set me up with their professors and some of their friends fathers; quite embarrassing really. Even Ben was convinced that I was dying on the vine and needed a male in my life. I accused him of just wanting me out of his house.

Today was a dreary, rainy, melancholy February day, a day that explains why they are called, "the February Doldrums." I was in the kitchen just taking a batch of oatmeal muffins out of the oven when the canine early warning system went off. Then I heard Allen telling Maggie to get her nose out of his pocket. I went out to the back porch to meet him. Ben came out of his office as well. Both boys were in their classes.

"That was timing," I said. "A batch of muffins is just out of the oven and there's a fresh pot of coffee."

"That sounds wonderful," he said stamping the rain and mud off himself before coming into the kitchen. "Oh go on with you now," he said to the dogs. I gave you all I had."

"What brings you all the way out here on a day like this?" I hope we aren't in violation of some petty ordinance," Ben chuckled.

"Nope. Nothing like that." He took a bite of a muffin. "Ooh! Hot! Hot!"

"I told you they were fresh out of the oven."

"I just dropped by with a bit of news."

"Oh?" I said.

"Yes, Ed Sloan was killed last night."

"What?" Ben and I exclaimed at once.

"Yep. Found drowned in the lavatory."

"Good God," Ben said. "And of course no one knows how it happened."

"That's right. An accident."

"Right," I said. "Like anyone can accidentally drown in the john."

"There are two things that cons won't tolerate," Allen said. "One is cruelty to animals. The other is pedophilia. Pedophilias are usually kept isolated from the other cons for their own safety. No one knows why Ed was put in a regular cellblock. The word is that he was hated by the cons and guards alike. Could be it was a bit of jailhouse justice."

"Well, I guess there's an end to it," I said. "Are you going to go tell the kids?"

"They have to be told. Their caseworker is going out to the Murdock's tomorrow. I doubt if she will tell them the exact details; just that their father is dead."

"How are the adoption procedures going?" I asked.

"They look good. The kids like it there, even the little girl. She has quit hiding. Mrs. Murdock has her in pre-school now and the littlest boy is in school too.

"That's wonderful news," I said as I poured Allen another cup of coffee.

"Jo has some good news too," Ben announced as he refilled his mug.

"Oh?" Allen asked, turning to me.

"It's nothing much really."

"Nothing much!" Ben spat. "Hell! She's just been given the California Cookbook author of the year award. That's all. Goes to a big shindig in San Francisco next week to receive it."

"Now that is good news," Allen said, "and it deserves a hug." He jumped from his chair and embraced me.

"She hasn't got a date yet," Ben said. I was so embarrassed I thought I could die and I'm sure Allen was to. He immediately released me, sat back down and took a sip of coffee.

"As a matter of fact, Sean is going to escort me."

"A priest isn't a date," Ben said. "Oh yes. She also just signed a contract for a new book. Our Jo is quite the catch for the right man..." he beat a fast retreat as I threw a hot-potholder at his head.

"That's great Jo," Allen said, having recovered from his embarrassment. "Is it another cookbook? What's it about?"

"Crab. All recipes for our wonderful local Dungeness crab. I'll need some willing guinea pigs to test the experiments."

"Ah, gee. Now that's a tough one Jo. I don't know if I can handle it or not." We laughed and he reached for another muffin.

Appendices

Jo's Recipes

Jo's Notes

Maps

The Recipes

Here are recipes for some of the dishes I have mentioned in this story. It seemed to me that it would be rather cruel to have to read about good food and not be able to try any of it. Some of the recipes are mine and some are those of my friends who happen to be fine cooks. My recipes are a mixture of those I created for my Zinfandel cookbook; others are just things my family loves. I benevolently have not included the recipe for Lacey's bean salad. Lacy is a good friend with many skills. Cooking is not one of them. There may be hope however. Despite her straight laced background she is becoming quite; as she calls it, *"Californicated."*

I have listed the recipes in the order in which they are mentioned in the book. Incidentally, for the Zinfandel recipes, if Zinfandel is not available in your area, you may substitute a robust, full-bodied red wine, on pain of death however, never use white Zinfandel. Oh yes, if you can't find a late harvest Zin, you may substitute Port; but not a white Port.

Recipes from Chapters 1 and 2

The following recipes are from my Guinea Pig Dinner. Hey, I didn't serve Guinea Pig, although it is a delicacy in some cultures; my guests were the Guinea Pigs.

My Three Cheese Tartlets
makes 24

> *If your family is like mine you will have to make far more of these than you need or there won't be any left to serve.*

The Pastry:

2 ½ cups all-purpose flour
1 cup (2 *sticks* or ½ *pound*) cold butter, lard, shortening or
    combination thereof
1 teaspoon white distilled vinegar
1 egg

Put flour in a large bowl. Cut the butter, lard or shortening into small pieces and add. Using an old fashion wire pastry blender work the fat into the flour until it is the texture of coarse cornmeal.

Put the vinegar and egg into a one-cup measure and blend well. Add enough cold water to bring the total amount of liquid to ½ cup. Make a well in the center of the flour-fat mixture and pour all of the liquid in at once. With a table fork, stir round and round until all of the flour mixture is moistened. Turn out onto a lightly floured surface and knead very gently, just enough to make all the bits and pieces cling together. Beware of over kneading or the resulting pastry will be tough. Form the dough into a ball and pat into a disk about one inch thick. Wrap in plastic and refrigerate while you make the filling.

Three Cheese Filling:

½ cup grated good Swiss cheese like Emmental or Gruyere
½ cup extra sharp Cheddar, preferably imported from England
½ cup finely crumbled blue cheese
2 cloves of fresh garlic, very finely minced
1 tablespoon finely minced fresh chives

3 large eggs
2 cups half and half or cream
½ teaspoon grated nutmeg
Salt and fresh coarse ground black pepper to taste
Paprika

Preheat the oven to 350°. *
Prepare the cheeses and toss gently with the minced garlic and cloves. Set aside. Beat the eggs and cream together, add the nutmeg, salt and pepper, stir well and set aside to allow any foam to subside.

Prepare 2½-inch muffin tins with non-stick spray and set aside. You will need enough to make twenty-four tarts. Remove the pastry from the refrigerator and working on a lightly floured surface, roll the dough to be no thicker than ¼ inch. **
Using a 3 inch round cutter, cut twenty-four circles of dough. Use these to line the muffin tins. Divide the prepared cheese mixture between the lined muffin tins. Spoon the egg/cream mixture, into the muffin tins. Carefully set the muffin tins in other baking pans and place in the middle of the oven. Fill the outer pans with enough hot water to come half way up the sides of the muffin tins. This *"water bath,"* provides the gentle heat necessary to keep the egg custard from curdling. Bake for about thirty to thirty-five minutes or until the custard is set. Use a slim bamboo skewer to test. Insert one into the center of a tartlet. If it comes out clean, the tartlets are done. Remove from the oven and allow to cool completely before trying to remove from the muffin tins.

A nice addition if your arteries can take it is a wee dollop of sour cream on top of each. Place on a serving tray and decorate with sprigs of parsley, fresh chives or other fresh herbs. These may be made the day before serving if you wish.

* When working with pastry, one usually wants to preheat the oven to the highest heat possible, 500° to 550°, and after the first few minutes of baking, turn the heat down to 350° however, when working with an egg custard filling, you need a gentle heat of the eggs will curdle.

** I am fortunate to be able to work in the kitchen of an old farmhouse. With the exception of installing certain modern connivances, Ben has left it alone, including one counter made of thick marble where I roll my pastry and knead my bread.

Zinfandel Terrine
makes one standard loaf pan

> *What's the difference between a "Terrine" and a "Pâté?"*
> *Today not much, however originally, a "Pâté" was encased*
> *in pastry and a "Terrine" was not.*

1-pound ground pork
2 chicken breasts, bone and skin removed and chopped very small
1/4 pound chicken livers, chopped very small
1 medium yellow onion, chopped small
6 to 8 cloves of garlic, minced
1 tablespoon dry mixed herbs, (*Italian seasoning*) or equivalent in
    minced fresh herbs
1/4 cup finely chopped fresh parsley
2 eggs, lightly beaten
1/2 teaspoon ground nutmeg
1 teaspoon fresh coarse ground black pepper to taste
Salt to taste
Thin sliced bacon
2 bay leaves *

1 1/2 cups Zinfandel
1/2 cup inexpensive cream Sherry
1/4 cup inexpensive brandy

Preheat oven to 325°. Mix the first eleven ingredients together well and set aside. Line a standard oblong loaf pan with bakers parchment, leaving about 4 inchers hanging over the long sides. This makes it easier to remove the terrine from the pan when finished. Next, line the pan with thin slices of bacon. Make a small patty of the meat mixture and sauté it in a skillet and taste. Adjust seasonings. Pack the meat mixture into the prepared loaf pan. Cover the top of the meat with bacon slices and lay the two bay leaves on top. Set the loaf pan in a larger pan and place in the center of the oven. Pour in enough hot water to come half way up the sides of the loaf pan. This *"water bath"* provides an even temperature necessary for a good texture. Bake for about two and a half to three hours.

Remove the baking pans from the oven and carefully pour off as much of the accumulated fat as possible. Empty the outer pan and set the loaf pan back in it. Mix the Zinfandel, Sherry and brandy together and pour about half of it over the terrine while it is still warm. Fold several thicknesses of aluminum foil to make a sort of lid that is the size of the top of the loaf pan. Set it on top of the terrine and put a weight on it. Leave cool but unrefrigerated place until completely cooled. Remove the foil and pour on a bit more of the wine mixture. Refrigerate. It is edible the next day, however I feel it will be far better if you age it for two to three days before serving. To age it, pour a little more of the wine mixture over it each day.

When ready to serve, remove from the loaf pan using the ends of the bakers' parchment to lift it out. Remove the parchment and place the terrine on a serving plate. Cut into thin slices and serve with baguette or brown bread, radishes and green onions.

* Most of you will have to use commercially available imported dry Mediterranean bay. I much prefer using fresh California Bay-Laurel. If you live in California, you can probably find someone with a bay tree who will let you pinch some. Pick a branch and hang it in your kitchen. You can use it for months.

Fresh Mushroom and Zin Soup with Garlic Snippets
serves 6

> *Please don't expect this delicious and delicate soup to bear any resemblance to the canned version; and no, you can't use it to make a tuna and noodle casserole.*

The Soup:

2 tablespoons olive oil
2 tablespoons butter
1 medium size yellow onion, diced
4 cloves of garlic, minced
½ pound fresh mushrooms, sliced thin (*if the mushrooms are large half them before slicing*)

6 cups of beef stock, broth or bouillon (*homemade or commercial*) *
Bouquet garni ** or 1 tablespoon dry mixed herbs (*Italian seasoning*)

1 cup Zinfandel
½ cup cream Sherry
1 teaspoon sugar or to taste
Salt and fresh coarse ground black pepper to taste

Garnish:

Fresh mushrooms
Sprigs of fresh herbs

Heat the olive oil and butter together in a large pot and gently sauté the onion and garlic until golden brown. Add the mushrooms and continue to sauté until translucent, about three to four minutes. Add the beef broth and the Bouquet garni, bring to a boil and immediately reduce the heat to maintain a rapid simmer. Simmer covered for twenty to thirty minutes. Add the wine, sugar, salt and pepper and simmer for another five minutes. Serve in a tureen or individual bowls. Garnish with a few slices of fresh mushroom and sprigs of fresh herbs. Serve hot accompanied by snippets of garlic toast.

* If using canned stock or broth, use 1, 49.5 or 3, 14.5-ounce cans.

** Using cotton twine, make a bundle of a sprig each of fresh rosemary, thyme, sage, oregano, celery tops and a bay leaf.

Garlic Toast Snippets:

1 stick, (*¼ pound or ½ a cup*) softened, not melted butter
4 to 6 cloves of minced garlic
¼ cup finely minced fresh parsley
French bread baguette

Grated Parmesan cheese

Mix the butter, garlic and parsley together. Slice the baguette into thin slices and spread with the butter mixture. Sprinkle lightly with the Parmesan and place on a wire rack set over a baking sheet. Place under the broiler and leave only until golden brown around the edges. Place in a basket lined with a clean cloth and serve hot

Coq a Zin
serves 4 to 6

> This is a delicious Sonoma county twist on the old Burgundian classic. My kids, punsters above and beyond the call of duty, named it.

1 large chicken cut into serving pieces *

1 cup all-purpose flour
1 tablespoon Herbs d'Provence **
1 teaspoon salt
1 teaspoon fresh coarse ground black pepper

2 to 3 strips of thick cut bacon, diced *(inexpensive bacon ends are best for this)*
Olive oil

1 large yellow onion, diced
4 to 6 cloves of garlic, chopped
1 stalk of celery, diced small
1 carrot, diced small

1 cup homemade or 1 can commercial chicken broth
Bouquet garni
1 cups Zinfandel
½ cup inexpensive cream Sherry
About a pound of pearl onions, peeled
About a pound of small mushrooms
Salt and fresh, coarse ground black pepper to taste
½ cup fresh chopped parsley

Cut the chicken into serving pieces. Put the flour, Herbs d'Provence, salt and pepper in a small paper bag and drop the chicken in, 2 or 3 pieces at a time, shake gently to coat with flour and set aside. Place the bacon in a heavy pot or large deep skillet, (*I use cast iron*) and gently sauté over a moderate heat. Do not let the bacon brown. You are just rendering the fat out of it. This will take 2 or 3 minutes. When the fat has been rendered, brown the chicken on all sides, in the fat, then set aside.

Over a moderate heat, gently sauté the onion, garlic, celery and carrot until softish. Do not allow to brown completely. Add the chicken broth and bouquet garni and bring to a boil. Reduce the heat to maintain a simmer. Return the chicken to the pot and add the Zinfandel and Sherry. Cover the pot with a lid and continue to simmer until the chicken is exceedingly tender, almost falling off the bones, about 45 minutes to an hour.

Meanwhile, prepare the onions and mushrooms and blanch.*** When the chicken is tender, add the blanched mushrooms and onions, and season to taste with salt and fresh coarse ground black pepper. Add the parsley and simmer only until the vegetables are hot through.

Place on a serving dish and surround with buttered fresh homemade egg pasta.

* Remove the legs and thighs and separate. Remove the breasts and cut each into two pieces. Cut back into 2 or 3 pieces and use, along with the giblets and neck to make stock. You may of course buy an already sectioned chicken.

** Herbs d'Provence is the same as Italian seasoning with the addition of fennel seeds and lavender blossoms

*** To blanch vegetables, bring a pot of water to the boil. When rapidly boiling, carefully slide the vegetables into it and cook briefly, then remove from the boiling water and immediately place in cold running water to completely cool as fast as possible. In the case of mushrooms, they should be removed as soon as the water returns to the boil. The onions should boil for about 1 minute only.

Fresh Handmade Pasta
makes 4 to 6 servings

> *If you've never made fresh handmade pasta you really should give it a try. Believe me, it's not rocket science.*

2 cups all-purpose flour
2 eggs
2 tablespoon olive oil
Water

Place flour, eggs and olive oil into a bowl and blend, adding just enough water to form into a soft yet kneadable dough. Turn the ball of dough out onto a lightly floured bowl and knead until smooth, glossy and somewhat elastic. Set aside and allow to rest for about 20 minutes.

When ready to form, divide the dough into four to six pieces and form into balls. One ball at a time, working on a lightly floured surface, roll the dough out to be about ¼ inch thick. Cut into broad noodles. You may use a knife or one of those crinkle-cutter wheels for pastry. To serve with this dish I like short, broad noodles, about two thirds of an inch by two inches. For things like pasta with clam sauce I like long noodles about one quarter inch wide.

When the noodles are cut, allow them to rest for about ten to twenty minutes before cooking. To cook, bring a large pot of water to the boil and carefully drop the noodles in. Cook for three or four minutes only. Drain but do not rinse. Toss with butter and serve. Sometimes I like to toss them with some minced fresh herbs like parsley, dill or chives.

Beef Medallions in Zinfandel Reduction with Braised Shallots
serves 4

O.K. For this one you are going to have to take a second on the house or sell the kids. You will need that incredibly expensive cut of meat, The Tenderloin. Tenderloin is that long narrow muscle lying lengthwise on either side of the spine of a mammal. It gets very little use so it is one of the tenderest cuts available. Since you're paying so much for the meat, go the whole hog and get a really great old growth Zinfandel to serve with it.

The Beef:

I to I ½ pounds lean beef Tenderloin

I cup Zinfandel
4 to 6 cloves of garlic, minced
½ large yellow onion, diced
I small sprig of fresh rosemary, bruised
I tablespoon sugar
½ teaspoon salt
I teaspoon fresh coarse ground black pepper
I tablespoon olive oil
I tablespoon sweet and hot brown mustard – (page 186)

I cup beef broth, stock or bouillon

Wipe the beef well on all sides and cut into half inch thick medallions. Set aside. Mix the next nine ingredients together in a bowl and add the medallions. Knead gently with your hands to insure that all parts of the beef are covered with the marinade, cover with plastic wrap and allow to marinate for about 2 hours.

Timing is essential for this dish. The meet is thin and will cook very quickly, therefore you need to have the reduction and the shallots prepared prior to broiling the beef medallions.

The Reduction:

Drain the marinade from the beef medallions, cover the meat and set aside. Strain the marinade and put in a deep, heavy skillet. Add the cup of beef broth and bring to a boil, stirring all the while. Allow to boil for about a minute. Reduce the heat to a rapid simmer and stirring frequently to prevent a skin from forming, cook until reduced by half. Set aside and keep warm. Move on the shallots.

The Shallots:

16 to 20 shallots, depending on size (choose evenly sized ones)
2 tablespoons of olive oil
½ cup Zinfandel
½ cup beef broth
¼ cup inexpensive cream Sherry
1 tablespoon sweet and hot brown mustard – (page 186)
Salt and fresh ground black pepper to taste

Peel the shallots. Heat the olive oil in a heavy skillet over a moderately high heat and add the shallots. Shake the pan frequently to keep the shallots moving and caramelize (brown) on all sides. When all the shallots are caramelized, add the wines, broth and mustard and stir well. Reduce heat to a rapid simmer and cook covered until the shallots are tender but not mushy. You should just be able to pierce them with a slim bamboo skewer. Remove the lid, increase the heat a bit and cook until most of the liquid has evaporated however you do not want the dish to be completely dry.

To Assemble:

Turn your oven to the highest broiler heat. Lay the beef medallions on your broiler pan and cook, turning once, to desired degree of doneness. They are best cooked briefly to a char-rare.

Lay the broiled medallions in a line down the center of an oval serving platter. Surround with the shallots. Quickly reheat the reduction and pour over the beef. Garnish with a sprig of fresh rosemary and serve immediately.

Carrots in Zin-Mustard Glaze
serves 4 to 6

This dish can make even the pickiest eater love his veggies.

3 or 4 carrots, cut into approximately ½ inch by 3 inch julienne

2 tablespoons butter
1 tablespoon olive oil
1 tablespoon sweet and hot brown mustard – *(page 186)*
½ cup Zinfandel
¼ cup cream Sherry
About 1 teaspoon minced fresh dill weed or ¼ teaspoon dry
A scant ¼ teaspoon grated nutmeg
Salt and fresh coarse ground black pepper to taste

Peel and cut the carrots and cook in boiling water to desired degree of doneness. Drain and put into cold running water immediately. Drain and set aside until needed.

Just before serving, melt the butter and olive oil together in a heavy skillet. Whisk in the mustard, wines and seasonings. Simmer, whisking all the while until somewhat thickened and sauce like. Add the carrots and toss them gently in the sauce until they are hot through. Place on a serving dish and garnish with sprigs of fresh dill weed or parsley. Serve hot.

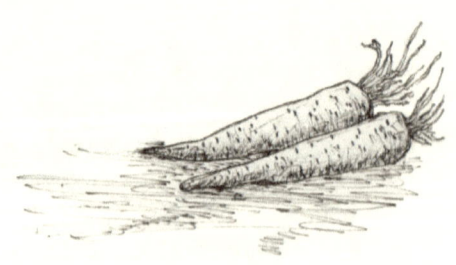

Broccoli with Parmesan
serves 4 to 6

> *This is a delicious and incredibly delicious way to serve broccoli, particularly if you don't cook it to death.*

About 5 cups of fresh broccoli florets

2 tablespoons butter
1 tablespoon olive oil
2 cloves of garlic, very finely minced

1/4 cup grated fresh Parmesan
Salt and fresh coarse ground black pepper to taste
6 to 8 small cloves of roasted garlic – (page 148)
Curls of fresh Parmesan

Blanch the broccoli florets in rapidly boiling water to desired degree of doneness. Remember, over cooked broccoli is a very sad thing. It should still have just a bit of tooth to it. Drain and plunge into cold running water immediately. When completely cold, drain and set aside until needed.

To serve, melt the butter and oil together and add the garlic. Swirl together until blended and add the blanched broccoli. Toss gently until the broccoli is heated and evenly coated with the butter/oil mixture. Sprinkle with the grated Parmesan, season to taste with salt and pepper and place in a serving dish. Top with curls of fresh Parmesan * and scatter on the roasted garlic cloves.

* To make curls, allow the cheese to come to room temperature, then use a vegetable peeler and "peel" off curls of cheese from a wedge. Your success will depend on the texture of the cheese. I have had cheeses that made beautiful perfect curls and others that made piles of sawdust.

Roasted Garlic
makes as much as you want

> O.K. So this isn't the way you see the T.V. chefs roast garlic. They roast the whole bulb in the oven and then squeeze it out of the husk to use it, right? I find that messy and wasteful. I think you will find my version easy to make and far more convenient to use. You may buy fresh garlic and peel the cloves, which is a significant pain, or buy the jars of ready peeled garlic cloves – way easier. Make as much or as little at a time as you want. I usually buy a pound jar and roast the whole thing. Refrigerated it will keep for a month or more.

Olive oil
Garlic

Using a large heavy skillet, (*cast iron is best*) wipe the bottom lightly with olive oil. Pour in enough peeled garlic cloves to cover the bottom one layer deep. Gently cook the garlic over a medium heat until evenly browned on all sides and soft. This will take about 15 to 20 minutes and should be done when you are going to be in the kitchen because you should not leave it. Turn the garlic frequently to prevent it from scorching. I do this by shaking the pan, however you may use a spatula or large, flat wooden spoon. When all the garlic is a pale golden brown, and soft enough that you can squash it, allow it to cool and then place in a jar or other covered container. Refrigerated it will keep for a long, long time.

This is so incredibly useful. There it is, ready to use in sauces, dressings, marinades, salads, pasta, veggies or
just to sprinkle with a tad of salt and
munch.

Apple-Walnut Salad with Zin-Cranberry Vinaigrette
serves 4 to 6

This is an unusual salad, perfect for Sonoma County which, in addition to premium wine grapes, also produces an excellent crop each year of beautiful Gravenstein apples.

The Vinaigrette:

1 cup sweetened dried cranberries, chopped
½ cup Zinfandel
¼ cup cranberry juice
¼ cup cider vinegar
¼ cup olive oil
2 cloves of garlic, sliced
1 sprig of fresh dill weed, bruised
Salt and fresh coarse ground black pepper to taste

Put all ingredients into a jar with a tight fitting lid, shake well and leave sit unrefrigerated over night. Strain to use. This will keep in the refrigerator indefinitely.

The Salad:

About 2 cups of torn Iceberg lettuce
About 2 cups of torn Romani lettuce
About 2 cups mixed spring salad mix
1 stalk of celery, chopped
About 3 crisp fresh apples, chopped with the peel on
½ a medium size sweet purple onion cut into thin rings
About ¾ cup chopped toasted walnuts

Salt and fresh coarse ground black pepper to taste

Toss all ingredients together gently in a large salad bowl. Drizzle over just enough of the vinaigrette to moisten and season to taste with salt and pepper. Toss again and serve chilled.

Pears with Blue Cheese and Late Harvest Zinfandel
per serving

> *This is an elegant and delicious dessert; a light and perfect ending to a rich meal, and it's so, so easy.*

½ a perfectly ripened pear
About 2 tablespoons crumbled blue cheese
About 2 tablespoons late harvest Zinfandel Port
Fresh coarse ground black pepper
Garnish

Choose large perfect pears, preferably Bartletts. Cut in half lengthwise but do not peel. Using a pear pitter if you have one, a spoon if you don't, remove the core from the pear. Place on an elegant dessert plate. Fill the hole in the pear with the crumbled blue cheese and scatter the remaining cheese over the pear and onto the plate. Drizzle about two tablespoons of Late Harvest Zinfandel Port over the pear. Finish with a grinding of fresh, coarse ground black pepper. Garnish with a sprig of fresh herb and an edible flower like a pansy or calendula.

Recipe from Chapter 3

Ma's Marvelous Munchable Muffins
makes 12, 2 ½ inch muffins

> *These are a basic streusel topped muffin and one of Lee's favorites. He even named them, gawd forbid!.*

2 cups all-purpose flour
1 tablespoon baking powder
¼ cup sugar
1 teaspoon powdered cinnamon
½ teaspoon powdered ginger
½ teaspoon ground nutmeg

2 eggs, lightly beaten
¼ cup vegetable oil or melted butter
1 cup water

Streusel topping – *(page 152)*
Bakers' syrup – *(page 153)*

Preheat oven to 375°. Prepare muffin tins with non-stick spray. Sift all dry ingredients together into a large bowl. Add the eggs, oil and water and mix just until dry ingredients are moistened.* Fill the muffin cups to about two-thirds full. Top each with about a tablespoon full of streusel topping. Put in the center of the oven and bake for 15 to 20 minutes or until a slim bamboo skewer inserted into the center of a muffin comes out clean.

Remove from the oven, place on a wire rack and immediately pour over each muffin about a tablespoon of warm bakers' syrup. Allow the muffins to sit in their tins for about five minutes before you try to remove them. Place in a basket lined with a clean cloth and serve hot with butter. My family can hardly start the day without fresh hot muffins.

* To achieve that characteristic pebbly texture, essential to a good muffin, it is important not to over mix. Over mixing will develop the gluten in the flour and cause you to have, not muffins but hockey pucks.

Streusel Topping:

This very handy topping can be made in quantity and kept in the freezer. It is useful to enhance muffins, coffee cakes and other baked goods. This recipe is a good way to start, however, you may also save any leftover sweet baked goods, like stale cake, cookies, muffins, coffee cake etc. crumble them, add butter, sugar and spices to taste and use it for streusel, which is exactly how streusel was invented by thrifty farmers wives.

2 cups flour
1 cup instant oatmeal
2 cups sugar
1 cup butter or margarine
2 tablespoons powdered cinnamon
1 tablespoon ground nutmeg
1 tablespoon powdered ginger
1 teaspoon ground cloves

Use your hands and mix everything together exceedingly well. You may keep this in the freezer for months.

Baker's Syrup
makes about 2 cups

>This simple syrup is an easy way to enhance many baked items.
>I try to never be without it.

1 ½ cups water
1 cup sugar
2 tablespoons butter or margarine
1 teaspoon vanilla extract

Put all ingredients together in a saucepan and bring to the boil. Reduce heat to maintain a simmer and cook for about fifteen minutes. This may be kept in a jar in the refrigerator and reheated when needed.

Recipes from Chapter 5

Gnocchi with Fresh Basil/Tomato Sauce *(without stilton)*
serves 4 to 6

> *Fresh hand-made gnocchi is a bit of a fiddle but it is so, so much better than any you will find in the market. When my kids were little they loved to help me form them. If you don't have time to make your own, you may still use this sauce with the commercial gnocchi.*

The Gnocchi:

1 large potato, boiled
1 large egg, lightly beaten
1 tablespoon olive oil
½ teaspoon grated nutmeg
All-purpose flour
Salt and pepper to taste

Boil the potato until tender. Drain, peel and run through a potato ricer, or fluff with a fork. Whip in the egg, oil and nutmeg, then begin adding flour until you achieve a soft dough. Knead until smooth. Set aside and allow to rest for about fifteen minutes.

When ready to form, cut dough into four to six pieces and form into balls. Gently roll the balls, one at a time into ropes about half an inch in diameter. With a sharp knife cut each rope into chunks about 1 inch long. Roll each small piece into a ball. Now, to make the characteristic ridged shape, press the back of a table fork into a small pile of flour, then roll the ball down the back of the fork, pressing gently. Yes, it's tedious but it's worth it when you hear your friends say, "No way! You didn't make these yourself."

Bring a large pot of water to the boil, reduce the heat to maintain a low, rolling boil and gently slide your gnocchi in. You are actually poaching them, not boiling them. Cook for three to five minutes or until they reach your desired degree of doneness.   Remember, handmade fresh pasta requires far less cooking time than dry commercial pasta. When done, drain but do not rinse. Return to the pot, toss with a bit of olive oil, cover and leave until ready to use.

Fresh Tomato/Basal Sauce

> *Whether served with fresh handmade gnocchi or commercial pasta this quick and easy chunky sauce brings the fresh tastes of high summer to your table. I'm sorry you won't be able to have some of Ben's excellent Zinfandel to enjoy with it.*

2 tablespoons olive oil
1 medium size yellow onion, diced
10 to 12 cloves of roasted garlic – (*page 148*) – coarsely chopped
4 to 6 large ripe tomatoes, chopped
1 tablespoon tomato paste
1 tablespoon sugar or to taste
½ cup Zinfandel
½ teaspoon ground nutmeg

1 cup chopped fresh basal leaves
Salt and fresh coarse ground black pepper to taste

Heat the olive oil in a heavy skillet and gently sauté the onion until golden brown and translucent. Add the garlic, tomatoes, tomato paste, sugar, wine and nutmeg and continue to sauté, stirring occasionally to prevent scorching until the tomatoes have released their juices and the whole has become somewhat thickened, about 10 minutes. This is a chunky sauce. Add the basal, salt and pepper, stir and simmer for another five minutes or so. Add the drained gnocchi or other pasta to the pan, stir gently and cook only until the pasta is reheated. Serve hot with a toss salad and fresh crusty Italian or French bread and a rich lusty Zinfandel.

Crumb Topped Coffee Cake
makes one 8 to 10 inch round coffee cake

You may follow the directions for my cake or cheat and use a box of spice cake mix and top it with streusel and enrich with bakers syrup.

1 ½ cups sugar
½ cup butter or margarine, softened
3 eggs

3 cups all-purpose flour
1 tablespoon baking powder
2 teaspoons powdered cinnamon
½ teaspoon ground nutmeg
½ teaspoon powdered ginger
¼ teaspoon ground cloves
About 2/3 cup of cold water

Streusel topping – (*page 152*)
Bakers' syrup – (*page 153*)

Preheat the oven to 350°. Prepare an eight to ten inch spring form pan with non stick spray. Cut a circle of bakers' parchment to place in the bottom. Cream the butter and sugar together until the sugar has dissolved. Whisk in the eggs. Sift the dry ingredients together. Add to the butter and sugar mixture and enough water to form a thick batter. Stir just until all lumps of flour are gone. Pour the batter into the prepared pan. Top with about a cup of streusel topping. Bake for thirty five to forty minutes or until a slim bamboo skewer inserted into the center comes out clean.

Remove from the oven and immediately pour about one cup of warm bakers' syrup evenly over the top. Allow to cool for about five minutes before slicing. This is excellent hot out of the oven or cold, but for a real treat, try it hot out of the oven with a bit of thick cream poured over. O.K., so you run a mile after or swim a dozen laps.

Harvest Time Pumpkin Spice Muffins
makes 12, 2 ½ inch muffins

These delicious muffins are my youngest son Jay's favorite.
They're rich and moist and the very essence of autumn.

2 cups all-purpose flour
   1 tablespoon baking powder
2 teaspoons powdered cinnamon
1 teaspoon powdered ginger
¼ teaspoon powdered cloves
1 cup sugar

1 cup pumpkin puree
2 eggs, lightly beaten
1 tablespoon dark molasses
¼ cup *(half a stick)* melted and cooled butter or margarine (or ¼ *cup*
   vegetable oil)
½ cup buttermilk
1 tablespoon vanilla flavoring

Streusel topping – *(page 152)*
Bakers syrup *(page 153)*

Preheat oven to 375°. Sift all dry ingredients together into a large
bowl. Add the wet ingredients and using as few strokes as possible,
stir only until most of the dry ingredients have been moistened.
Over mixing will produce hockey pucks, not muffins. Coat muffin
tins with non stick spray and fill each cup two-thirds full. Put about
one tablespoon of streusel topping on top of each muffin and place in
the center of the oven. Bake for twenty-five to thirty minutes or
until a slim bamboo skewer inserted in the center comes out clean.
Remove from the oven and immediately enhance with warm Baker's
syrup; about a tablespoon full drizzled over each muffin. Allow
muffins to sit in their pans for a few minutes before removing to a
basket or bowl lined with a clean cloth.

Zinfandel Muffins
makes 12, 2 ½ inch muffins

> *These muffins were an experiment for my Zinfandel cookbook. They have since become a family favorite; particularly during the crush when Ben and the boys are bring in the bins of grapes. Be prepared. The wine gives them a rather strange color.*

2 cups all-purpose flour
1 tablespoon baking powder
1 cup sugar
½ teaspoon powdered nutmeg

1 cup seedless red grapes
¼ cup vegetable oil or melted and cooled butter
2 eggs, lightly beaten
½ cup Zinfandel

Preheat oven to 375°. Sift all dry ingredients together into a large bowl. Add the wet ingredients and using as few strokes as possible, stir only until most of the dry ingredients have been moistened. Remember, over mixing produces tough muffins with an unappealing texture. Coat muffin tins with non-stick spray and fill each cup about three-quarters full. Bake for twenty to twenty-five minutes or until a slim bamboo skewer inserted in the center comes out clean. Allow to sit in the muffin tins for a few minutes before trying to remove. Place in a basket lined with a clean cloth and serve while still hot with lots of butter.

Recipes from Chapter 9

Homemade Frozen Pizza

> *My guys are real pizza hounds. What kids aren't? They call for pizza at the drop of a hat. I found it makes things a lot easier if I keep the makings in the freezer; portions of dough and plastic containers of homemade sauce. I try never to use commercial sauce because at Ben's age he shouldn't have that much sodium. Just read the labels. You'll be shocked at the amount of sodium in canned products.*

The Dough:

makes enough for 4, 10-inch pizzas or 2 loaves of bread or combination thereof

This is a basic white yeast dough that can be used for pizza, bread, bread sticks, rolls or buns. It will make enough dough for four ten inch pizzas, two medium size loaves of bread or any number of bread sticks and buns or rolls. For bread I usually use the dough fresh, however for pizza I often divide the dough into quarters, flatten each into a disk about 1 inch thick, wrap it in plastic and freeze it. I then have the makings for pizza any time my guys ask for it.

The Ferment:

½ cup warm water
¼ cup sugar
1 tablespoon dry active yeast

Put all ingredients into a small bowl and stir well. Set aside in a warm place for 15 to 20 minutes or until the mixture is frothy and bubbling a bit.

The Sponge:

The Ferment plus,
3 cups all-purpose flour
2 ½ cups warm water

Mix the flour and water together in a large bowl and add the ferment. Mix well, cover with a clean cloth or plastic and leave in a warm place until the mixture is "spongy" and bubbling. This will probably take from 30 minutes to an hour.

The Dough:

About ½ to 1 teaspoon of salt, depending on taste
About 4 to 5 cups of all-purpose flour

When the sponge is "working," add the salt and begin adding add the flour, one cup at a time and stirring well after each addition. When the mixture is too stiff to stir, turn it out onto a lightly floured surface and begin kneading and adding the remaining flour until you have a firm yet malleable dough. Knead until all stickiness is gone and the dough is smooth and glossy. Form into a ball and place in a clean lightly oiled bowl. Cover with a clean cloth or plastic and leave in a warm place until it has risen to double its original bulk. Punch it down, turn it over and allow to rise a second time. The amount of time it will take to rise will vary greatly depending on climate and temperatures.

Forming into Pizza:

After the second rising, turn the tough out onto a lightly floured surface and knead very lightly. For pizza, cut into four equal portions and roll out into flat disks about one quarter inch thick to fit your pizza pans. Add sauce and toppings and bake at 500° for 15 to 20 minutes or until the pizza is done to your liking. My guys like it extra crisp.

If you plan to freeze all or some of the dough, divide the dough into quarters and pat each into a disk about 1 inch thick. Wrap each in plastic and freeze. To thaw, remove from the freezer and leave on the counter at room temperature until thawed. DO NOT put in the microwave.

Forming Into Bread:

Form into one large or two smaller round or oblong loaves. Paint the surface with egg wash, *(an egg beaten with 1 tablespoon of cold water)* and with the tip of a sharp knife or a razor blade make several shallow slits in the top of each loaf. Place the loaves on baking sheets lined with baker's parchment and leave until nearly double in size.

Place the risen loaves in a pre-heated 350° oven and bake until golden brown, about thirty-five minutes for smaller loaves, forty-five to fifty minutes for one large loaf. For a crisp crust, allow to cool while sitting on wire racks. For a soft crust, wrap in a clean cloth and allow to cool.

Red Sauce:

2 to 3 tablespoons olive oil
2 yellow onions, diced
15 to 20 cloves of garlic, chopped
1 bell pepper, seeded and diced
1 stalk of celery, diced

About 2 pounds fresh tomatoes, diced, or 3, 14.5-ounce cans of
    diced tomatoes
1 tablespoon mixed dry herbs, *(Italian seasoning)* or favorite fresh
    herbs
2 tablespoons red wine vinegar, or to taste
2 tablespoons sugar, or to taste
¼ cup Zinfandel or other full bodied red wine
Salt and fresh coarse ground black pepper to taste

Heat the olive oil in a large heavy pot. Add the onions, garlic, bell pepper and celery and sauté until caramelized (*browned*) and softened. Add the tomatoes and continue to cook over a medium heat for about ten minutes. Add the remaining ingredients except salt and pepper and continue cooking, stirring occasionally to prevent scorching until the sauce is thickened, about twenty to thirty minutes. About half way through the cooking, add salt and pepper to taste. Also adjust the seasonings. You may wish to add a bit more vinegar and sugar. If you wish a smooth sauce, use an immersable blender and purée. We prefer our sauce a bit on the chunky side. You may use fresh or divide it into portions and freeze to have ready to hand to turn into pizza or to serve with pasta.

Recipes Chapter 10

Recipes for my Yuppie Ladies Class:

These are the Zinfandel dishes I tried out on my ladies from San Francisco. It was decided they were all keepers and so I included them in my cookbook. I hope you will enjoy them as well.

Buena Vista Meat Balls with Blue Cheese Polenta
serves 4 to 6

> *I dubbed this tasty dish Buena Vista Meat Balls because according to legend, Zinfandel wine was first produced at the Buena Vista Winery by Agoston Haraszthy.*

The Polenta:

Making polenta isn't rocket science but it is a bit tedious. Fresh homemade polenta is however, well worth the trouble.

3 cups boiling water
About 2/3 cup dry polenta or coarse ground corn meal
About 1/4 pound crumbled blue cheese
1 tablespoon chopped chives
Salt and fresh coarse ground black pepper to taste

Bring the water to a rolling boil. Using your fingers, begin slowly sprinkling the polenta or cornmeal into the boiling water, while continuously mixing with a large wooden spoon. When all the polenta or cornmeal has been added, reduce the heat to medium low and continue to stir until the mass comes away from the sides of the pot when stirring. Gently stir in the crumbled blue cheese and the chives and season to taste with salt and pepper. Pour out onto a lightly oiled flat surface and smooth the top so that mass will be about 1/2 inch thick. Allow to set. When set cut into squares or cut into rounds with a biscuit cutter. You may serve as is or fry in olive oil until lightly browned on both sides.

The Meat Balls:

2 tablespoons olive oil
1 yellow onion, chopped small
4 to 6 cloves of garlic, minced
1 teaspoon mixed dry herbs – (*Italian seasoning*)
1 pound lean ground beef
½ pound ground pork
1 cup cooked long grain rice
2 raw eggs, lightly beaten
½ teaspoon dry chili flakes, or to taste
1 teaspoon paprika
¼ cup finely chopped fresh parsley
1 teaspoon sugar
Salt and fresh coarse ground black pepper to taste

Olive oil for frying

Heat the olive oil in a heavy skillet and gently sauté the garlic, onions and herbs together until the onions are lightly caramelized, (*golden brown*). Allow to cool. Place all ingredients including the cooled onion mixture into a large mixing bowl and using your hands, mix thoroughly. Make a small patty and gently fry it to test for seasonings. Adjust the seasonings. Using your hands, form into small balls about the size of a walnut or golf ball.

To cook, heat one or two tablespoons of olive oil in a heavy skillet and over a moderate heat, gently sauté the meatballs until evenly browned on all sides. Remove from the pan and set aside.

Buena Vista Sauce:

3 tablespoons olive oil
4 to 6 shallots, very finely minced
3 or 4 cloves of garlic, very finely minced
2 tablespoons all-purpose flour

2 cups homemade or 1 - 14.5-ounce commercial beef stock or broth
1 cup Zinfandel
¼ cup cream sherry
2 teaspoons Sweet and Hot Brown Mustard – (page 186)
1 teaspoon dry mixed herbs – (Italian seasoning)
1 bay leaf
1 cup heavy cream
Salt and fresh coarse ground black pepper to taste

1 cup lightly sautéed fresh mushrooms, or more to taste

Heat the olive oil in a heavy skillet and gently sauté the shallots and garlic until pinkish and translucent. Sprinkle the flour over and stir in with a wooden spoon until well incorporate and just beginning to brown. Switch to a wire whisk and add the stock, whisking all the while. When thoroughly blended and slightly thickened, whisk in the wines and mustard. Add the bay leaf and simmer for about ten or fifteen minutes, or until translucent and somewhat reduced. Remove the bay leaf. Pour in the cream, whisk and season to taste with salt and pepper. Bring to a boil, whisking all the while and immediately reduce the heat to maintain a simmer. Add the mushrooms and the meat balls and simmer until the meat balls are heated through. Serve over polenta or fresh pasta – (page 142).

Arugula and Fresh Mushroom Salad with Zinfandel Vinaigrette
serves 4 to 6

> *Arugula has a unique flavor. It can be rather harsh tasting. When shopping for it, try to find the smallest you can with leaves no more than about three inches long. When it is larger it is usually older and a bit on the harsh side. The best Arugula is that which you grow yourself. It is very easy to grow and it is a "cut and come again," green. You can even grow it in a container.*

The Vinaigrette:

½ cup Zinfandel
¼ cup red wine vinegar
1/3 cup olive oil
2 teaspoons Sweet and Hot Brown Mustard – *(page - 186)*
1 shallot, finely minced
Salt and fresh coarse ground black pepper to taste

Combine all ingredients and whisk together. Put in a jar and set aside until needed.

The Salad:

3 cups of fresh Arugula
2 cups of sliced small raw mushrooms
About 20 edible pod peas
Thinly sliced rings from ½ a medium size sweet purple onion
1 cup pitted black olives, crushed but not chopped
1 cup garlic croutons

Toss all together and chill until ready to serve. Moisten with the vinaigrette just before serving. Serve chilled.

Late Harvest Zinfandel Sorbet
serves 4 to 6

> *You may make this delectable, light and refreshing dessert with or without an ice cream maker. Find a rich, late harvest Zinfandel. If you can't find one use half port and half Burgundy.*

1 cup water
1 cup sugar
juice of 1 lime

3 cups Zinfandel

Put water, sugar and lime-juice in a sauce pan and simmer until the sugar is completely dissolved. Cool, then add the wine and stir. If using an ice cream maker, follow the manufacturer's directions. To make in your freezer, pour the mixture into a shallow pan and freeze until a rim of ice about quarter inch thick forms on the bottom and around the sides of the pan. Remove the pan and with a fork, stir the ice crystals into the liquid and return to the freezer. Continue to do this until the entire mass is frozen. Once this process is complete you may remove the sorbet to a container and keep in the freezer until needed. Dish up with an ice cream scoop and serve in dessert dishes garnished with a slice of lime and a sprig of fresh mint.

If you allow the mixture to freeze without stirring in the ice crystals as they form it will freeze into a solid mass that is unusable.

Sinful Zinfull Brownies
makes 16 squares

> O.K. So this may sound like a real strange one, but hey, a lot of people like to eat chocolate with a full bodied red wine like Zinfandel. Now, I'm going to let you in on a little secret. I cheat. I use a mix. For years I struggled with brownies and I made lots of batches of really good tasting chocolate things, but to me they weren't classic brownies with that wonderful gooey texture and the glossy-crackly top.

To make these absolutely sinful delights, follow the directions on the box, replacing the water with Zinfandel and adding half a cup chopped Pecans. You are going to be surprised by how wonderful they are, and when people start applauding, don't tell them you used a mix.

Recipes from Chapter 12

The O'Malley's harvest festival is an event looked forward to with great anticipation each year. The music is always great, the wine excellent, the company stimulating and the food sensational and an amazing cultural hodgepodge.

Mrs. O'Malley's Paprikash and Späetzle
serves 4 to 6

> *I had quite a time reducing this recipe to produce a quantity small enough for the average family. Mrs. O'Malley said she had never made a batch that required fewer than a dozen chickens and an entire can of paprika. You may serve it with egg noodles, however I have included Mrs. O'Malley's recipe for traditional Späetzel, those magnificent tiny dumplings, cooked in rich chicken broth, so loved in Eastern European cuisine. Mrs. O'Malley's original recipe is not particularly heart-healthy, therefore I have made it a bit more so by substituting olive oil for the bacon drippings she uses.*

The Paprikash:

1 chicken cut into serving pieces or the equivalent in legs and thighs
½ cup all-purpose flour
2 tablespoons paprika
1 tablespoon garlic powder
1 tablespoon mixed dry herbs (*Italian seasoning*)
1 teaspoon salt
1 teaspoon fresh coarse ground black pepper

3 to 4 tablespoons olive oil
1 large yellow onion, diced
10 to 12 cloves of garlic, chopped
2 red ripe bell peppers, seeded and cut into strips

2 tablespoons paprika

1 teaspoon sugar

2 cups homemade or 1, 14.5-ounce can commercial chicken broth or
   stock

½ cup red wine (of course Mrs. O'Malley uses Zinfandel)

1 sprig fresh rosemary

1 bay leaf

Salt and fresh coarse ground black pepper to taste

¼ cup minced fresh parsley

1 cup sour cream

Späetzle (page 171) or the fresh Hand-made Pasta listed on (page
   142)

Section the chicken, rinse it under cold running water and pat dry.
Put the next 6 ingredients into a plastic bag and shake to mix. Add
the chicken a few pieces at a time and shake gently to coat evenly.
Set aside.

Heat the olive oil in a heavy skillet, (an old deep cast iron one is best)
sauté the vegetables until they are just beginning to brown around
the edges and are beginning to soften. Remove from the skillet with
a slotted spoon. Add a bit more olive oil if necessary and brown the
chicken, several pieces at a time, turning to cook evenly on all sides.
Using a pair of tongs, remove the chicken from the skilled and set
aside with the vegetables. Add the paprika, sugar and 1 tablespoon
of the flour to the skillet and stir over a moderate heat until the flour
is lightly browned. Slowly add the chicken stock, whisking all the
while. Add the wine and continue whisking until the mixture is
smooth, translucent and somewhat thickened. Return the chicken
and vegetables to the pan, add the rosemary and bay leaf, reduce the
heat to a simmer and cover with a tight fitting lid. Cook until the
chicken is your desired degree of doneness. Mrs. O'Malley cooks it

almost off the bone. When the chicken is done, season to taste with salt and pepper. Whisk in the parsley and sour cream, cover, turn off the heat and leave sit while you make the Späetzel or pasta.

The Späetzle:

2 cups all-purpose flour
2 eggs, lightly beaten
About ¾ cup water

Chicken stock, broth or bouillon

Mix the flour and egg together with enough water to form into a very soft dough or very thick batter. Bring about a quart of stock, broth or bouillon to the boil (*you may also use water*), reduce the heat to maintain a rapid simmer. You will now drop the dough-batter by very small droplets into the liquid. There are several ways to do this. First there is a tool available on the market and internet called a Späetzle Hex or Wizard that makes späetzle making very easy. If you don't have one, you may use a colander with holes about ¼ inch in diameter. Put a generous tablespoon of the batter into the colander, hold it over the pot of simmering broth and using a wooden spoon or rubber spatula, force the batter through the holes. The batter will drop into the broth in small droplets and form tender little dumplings. When the späetzle return to the top of the pot, simmer for about 2 more minutes, then remove from the pot with a slotted spoon and set aside in a bowl to keep warm while you cook the remaining batter. These delicious, tender little dumplings may be served on their own with butter or with a dish like this Paprikash. They are often served with sauerbraten.

Ross's Cornish Pasties

For all her urbanity, Ross is a country girl at heart, having been born on a farm near the quaint fishing village of Mousehole, (pronounced Mowzel) in Cornwall. She didn't move off the farm until she joined the RAF in WWII. She was taught how to make pasties by her "gran," (grandmother) on the farm.

Your favorite pastry
About 2 cups of cold beef gravy

1 ½ to 2 pounds of beef, *(chuck, flank and round are good choices)*
2 to 3 medium size potatoes
1 large onion or leek or combination thereof
1 small rutabaga or turnip
1 teaspoon mixed dry herbs – *(Italian seasoning)*, or favorite fresh
   herbs, minced
¼ cup chopped fresh parsley
Salt and fresh, coarse ground black pepper to taste
Egg wash – *(1 raw egg beaten with 1 tablespoon of cold water)*

Make the pastry and chill for about thirty minutes before using. Next make your gravy and allow it to cool thoroughly. Chop the meat into one-quarter inch dice. Peel the potatoes and dice. Dice the onion and or leek. If using leeks, be sure to include some of the green part, rinsed well to remove any dirt. Peel and dice the rutabaga. Combine the meat, vegetables, herbs, parsley, and cold gravy. Season to taste with salt and pepper. To check for seasoning put a bit on a dish and microwave for about a minute or two. Taste and adjust the seasonings.

Preheat the oven to 500°. Divide the pastry in half and roll to approximately one-quarter inch thick. Cut into rounds that are about six inches in diameter. Paint the outer rim of each circle with egg wash. Put about one-half cup of the meat and vegetable mixture in a line down the center of the circle of pastry. Be careful not to get any on the outer rim or the pasties will be very difficult to seal. Fold the pastry in half to form a turnover and crimp to seal well. You may leave them this way, or position the pasty so that the crimped seal is across the top. Place on a baking pan that has been lined with baker's parchment. Continue forming remaining pasties. Place them about one inch apart on the baking sheets. Paint each pasty with the egg wash and using a small sharp knife, made two small slits about one half inch long in the top of each pasty. Place in the preheated 500° oven for five minutes, then reduce the heat to 350° and bake for an additional thirty-five to forty-five minutes or until the pastry is a beautiful golden brown and the kitchen smells heavenly. Pasties are excellent hot or cold.

Alberto's Mother's Guacamole
makes about 2 to 3 cups

I make good Guacamole, however Alberto's mothers is the best I have ever had. I have cut her recipe down to workable size. She usually makes it by the bath tub full.

3 or 4 very ripe avocados
The juice of 2 fresh limes
1 small yellow onion diced very small
2 or 3 cloves of garlic, finely minced
1 green onion, chopped small including the greens
1 small Jalapeño chili, seeded, white pith removed and what remains
    chopped fine
About 2 tablespoons finely chopped cilantro
Salt and fresh coarse ground black pepper to taste

Mix all ingredients together well. Cover with plastic and allow to rest for about thirty minutes. Taste and adjust seasonings. You may wish to add a bit more lime and pepper. This is excellent as a dip or as an accompaniment to burritos, tacos and the like. Hey, my kids use it to make sandwiches.

Recipes from Chapter 17

Sonoma Zinfandel Pot Roast
serves 4 to 6

> *My guys love pot roast. It's a dish I usually reserve for those days when the weather turns chill, but so, I had to experiment for my book despite the fact that autumn in Sonoma is often hotter than the proverbial hinges of hell. You might think a 4 to 5 pound roast a bit much for 4 to 6 servings. Believe me, nothing is better that sandwiches made from left over pot roast.*

The Roast:

1, 4 to 5 pound bone in chuck roast
3 to 4 tablespoons olive oil

2 large yellow onions, diced
6 to 8 cloves of garlic, chopped
1 carrot, scraped and diced
1 rib of celery, chopped
1 green bell pepper, seeded and chopped

1 cup Zinfandel
2 cups homemade or 14.5-ounce can commercial beef broth, stock
   or bouillon
1 bay leaf
1 sprig each fresh rosemary, sage, thyme, savory and oregano or 2
   tablespoons mixed dry herbs – (Italian seasoning)
1 tablespoon sugar

Pre-heat oven to 325°. Trim any large pieces of fat off the roast. Heat the olive oil in a large heavy ovenproof pot with a tight fitting lid. Brown the meat well on all sides. Remove the meat to a plate and set aside. Add the next five ingredients to the pot and gently sauté until the onions are translucent, pinkish and just beginning to brown around the edges. This mixture of vegetables is called a *Mirepoix* and is often used to add flavor to stocks, broths, soups and stews. Return the meat to the pot, add the wine, broth, herbs and sugar and bring to a boil. Cover with a tight fitting lid and place in the center of the oven. Cook for about two and a half to three hours or until the meat is exceedingly tender. Check occasionally. You may have to add a bit more broth from time to time.

Here's a little tip, whenever you are oven cooking meat or chicken, cover the bottom of the pan with thick slices of onion and then set your roast or chicken on them. This will prevent the meat from scorching on the bottom, plus adding additional flavor.

The Vegetables:

While the meat is cooking, prep your vegetables. I know, your standard pot roast has potatoes, carrots and perhaps green beans. I like to break from tradition on occasion. This version utilizes summer vegetables and instead of potatoes, I serve it with fresh gnocchi – (page 154).

1 pound of small boiling onions, peeled
2 sweet red peppers, seeded and cut into strips
2 Anaheim chilies, cut into rings
½ pound small mushrooms
2 to 3 zucchini, cut into ¼ inch thick slices
About 6 Roma tomatoes, cut in half and the stem end removed

These are tender summer vegetables and you don't want to cook the life out of them. Instead of cooking them along with the roast in the traditional manner, you will add them to the roast near the end of its cooking time. When the roast is nearly ready, add the vegetables and cook until they are tender, about thirty minutes.

To Serve:

Form your gnocchi while the roast is cooking. When you add the vegetables to the pot, begin poaching your gnocchi. When the gnocchi is done, drain it and toss with a bit of butter and fresh chopped parsley.

To serve, place the roast on a serving platter and arrange the vegetables and gnocchi around it. Skim off excess fat from the pan juices and strain into a gravy boat or sauce dish. Serve with the roast and vegetables.

Recipes from Chapter 19

Do It Yourself Kebabs
can serve any number you wish

You might consider this recipe a bit of a cop-out. It's not really a recipe, just a suggestion. It's also a cop-out for the cook. All you have to do is chop the meat and veggies and chuck them into a bowl of marinade. Your guests assemble and cook their own skewer.

A word about kebabs. We, in the western world use the work incorrectly. Kebab does not necessarily mean food cooked on a skewer. It is a term for meat quickly cooked. There are many types of kebabs including the classic "Sis Kebab." The skewer the meat and veg are threaded onto is a "sis." Now, with that bit of information you might win a trivia competition.

Traditionally Kebab is made with lamb, however in the states it has come to be anything you can thread onto a skewer or "sis" and place over hot coals. Lamb is excellent but beef is good as well. I'd stay away from pork because there is a chance that it won't be done enough before the vegetables are cooked to a cinder. You can use chicken cut from the bone, seafood like prawns and scallops, and even organ meats. The Greeks are very fond of using organ meats on their sis.

If you are planning to make Sis Kebab for a large gathering, I suggest you use any of the following or a combination thereof:

Appropriate Meats:

Cubed Lamb
Cubed Beef
Off the bone chicken
Cubed organ meats
Peeled prawns
Scallops
Cubed firm fleshed fish like shark or swordfish
Kielbasa
Cubed goat meat
and for those of you who have avid hunters in the family:
   Venison, Wild Boar or Elk

Appropriate Vegetables:

Small par-boiled boiling onions
Bell pepper chunks: green, red, yellow or orange
Anaheim or Italian roasting peppers
Summer squash chunks: zucchini, crook-neck or patty-pan
Eggplant chunks
Cherry tomatoes
Mushrooms of choice
Chayote
Cauliflower florets
Broccoli florets
Par-boiled new potatoes
Cubes of winter squash of choice

Cut meats and vegetables into sizes and shapes of choice, place in large bowls and cover with favorite marinades. I have listed my Zinfandel marinade below. I find it a good idea to keep your meats, seafood and vegetables in separate bowls. Cover the bowls with plastic wrap until needed.

If you are using disposable bamboo skewers, soak them in water for about an hour before using. This helps to keep them from incinerating when placed on the grill. Incidentally, if you have a large upright, (*not a trailing*) rosemary plant, cut some of the straight twigs, strip off the leaves and use the twigs as skewers. They will flavor the meat from the inside out.

Once you have everything prepared all you have to do is sit back with a nice glass of wine and let your guests have at it.

Zinfandel Marinade
Makes one quart

1 large yellow onion, cut into thin rings
15 to 20 cloves of garlic, crushed
1 sprig of fresh rosemary
2 tablespoons sweet and hot brown mustard - (*page 186*)
½ cup olive oil
½ cup inexpensive cream Sherry
½ cup apple juice
½ cup soy sauce
2 cups Zinfandel
2 tablespoons Worcestershire sauce
Salt and fresh coarse ground black pepper to taste
Dry chili flakes to taste

Combine all ingredients, mix well and pour over meats or vegetables to be grilled. Allow to marinate for several hours. Brush items with marinade occasionally while they grill.

Recipes from Chapter 20

Stuffed Game Hens in Zinfandel Glaze
serves 4

> *Game hens are an excellent and inexpensive way to add a touch of elegance to any meal. Stuff them and finish with a delectable glaze and they become even more elegant. What's wrong with gilding the lily once in a while? This recipe is one of the keepers that wound up in my Zinfandel cookbook.*

2 Cornish game hens – about 20-ounces each

If frozen allow the game hens to thaw completely, and remove the neck and giblets. Place in a small pot, with a clove of garlic and a pinch of mixed dry herbs, (Italian seasonings) cover with cold water, bring to a boil, then reduce the heat to a rapid simmer, cover and continue to cook until the giblets are very tender and the meat is falling off the bone. Rinse well inside and out, pat dry and set aside.

The Stuffing:

2 tablespoons olive oil
1 medium size yellow onion, diced
2 to 3 cloves of garlic, minced
1 teaspoon dry mixed herbs, (Italian seasoning)
½ teaspoon dry dill weed
½ teaspoon ground nutmeg
¼ teaspoon ground cardamom
¼ teaspoon ground cumin
1 teaspoon curry powder

3 cups cooked long grain white rice
The meat from the necks and giblets, chopped very fine
2 tablespoons currants

2 tablespoons pine nuts
2 tablespoons finely chopped crystallized ginger
1 teaspoon sugar, or to taste
Salt and fresh coarse ground black pepper to taste
¼ cup minced fresh parsley

1 egg, lightly beaten

Cook your rice by whatever method you prefer. When done it should still be al-dente, or still have a bit of "tooth" to it. Remember that since it will be cooked again inside the game hen, if it is completely cooked to begin with, the stuffing will be soggy. Set the rice aside and allow to cool.

Heat the olive oil in a heavy skillet and sauté the onion and garlic until the onion is pinkish and translucent. Add the next six ingredients and continue cooking over a moderate for another minute or so. Add the rice and next four ingredients and continue to cook, stirring until gently until well mixed. Season to taste with salt and pepper and stir in the parsley. Cool, then stir in the egg. Cover and set aside until needed.

The Glaze:

The strained broth from cooking the necks and giblets
1 cup Zinfandel
1 tablespoon sweet and hot brown mustard
2 tablespoons red currant jelly
½ teaspoon dry dill weed
About half a small yellow onion, chopped
1 clove of garlic, chopped

Put all ingredients into a pot, stir and bring to the boil. Reduce the heat to a rapid simmer, and whisking frequently, cook for two or three minutes. Strain. Return the liquid to the pot and cook until reduced by half its original volume. Taste and add salt and pepper if you wish.

To Assemble:

Preheat the oven to 350°. Wipe the game hens and fill the body cavities with the stuffing. Truss them shut with skewers or tooth picks. Place on a roasting rack and paint with olive oil. Place on the center rack of the oven and roast for approximately forty-five minutes, or until done to your desired degree of doneness. Paint frequently throughout the roasting with the glaze. Allow the game hens to cool for about five minutes before cutting them in half and arranging on a serving platter with their stuffing in piles beside them. Garnish with sprigs of fresh parsley or other fresh herbs.

Figs Poached in Zinfandel
serves 4

3 cups of Zinfandel
1 cinnamon stick
1 slice of fresh ginger root
3 tablespoons of sugar
The juice of one orange
2 or 3 strips of orange peel

8 to 14 large perfect black figs

Put the first six ingredients into a pot and bring to a boil. Reduce the heat and over a moderate heat, maintain a rapid simmer for about five minutes. Strain. Return to the pan and add the figs. Simmer until the figs well saturated with the liquid, about 10 minutes. Turn off the heat and allow the figs to sit in the syrup until cold. Remove the figs to individual serving dishes, three to four per person. Return the remaining syrup to the stove and cook until reduced by about half and somewhat thickened. Drizzle over the figs. These are extremely good served with a scoop of French vanilla ice cream or a slice of pound cake or hell, why not both.

Recipe from the Epilogue

Oatmeal-Raisin Muffing
Makes 12

> *To me, nothing says "Good morning," like a batch of fragrant muffins straight from the oven, and spicy oatmeal-raisin are some of my favorites.*

2 cups flour
1 cup quick cooking oatmeal
1 cup sugar
1 tablespoon baking powder
2 teaspoons powdered cinnamon
1 teaspoon ground nutmeg
½ teaspoon powdered ginger
¼ teaspoon powdered clove

1 cup raisins
2 eggs, lightly beaten
¼ cup vegetable oil or melted butter
1 cup buttermilk

Baker's syrup – *(page 153)*

Preheat the oven to 375°. Prepare 2 ½-inch muffin tins with nonstick spray. Sift all dry ingredients together into a large bowl. Toss the raisins with the dry ingredients. Add the eggs, oil or butter and buttermilk. Using as few strokes as possible, stir with a large wooden spoon only until all ingredients are moistened. Fill the muffin tins to about three-quarters full. Place in the center of the oven and bake for about 15 minutes or until a slim bamboo skewer inserted into the center comes out clean. Remove from the oven and immediately pour about a tablespoon of warm baker's syrup over each muffin. Allow to sit in the muffin tin for about five minutes before trying to remove. Serve warm in a basket lined with a clean cloth.

Sweet and Hot Brown Mustard
makes about 3 cups

Here is a bonus recipe. It's really delectable as a condiment and as an ingredient. Try mixing a bit of it with olive oil or butter, roasted garlic and cream Sherry in a skilled and pouring it over pasta or steamed vegetables as a quick and delicious sauce. On a Polish sausage sandwich it's tops.

½ cup brown mustard seeds
½ cup yellow mustard seeds
1 cup yellow mustard powder
1 cup sugar
Cider vinegar as needed

Put mustard seeds into the jar of a blender and pulse until they are cracked but not completely pulverized. Place in bowl with the mustard powder and sugar. Add as much cider vinegar as is needed to achieve the texture you want. Put into jars and store. This does not need to be refrigerated and will keep on a pantry shelf for months. As it sits, it will thicken. It can be thinned by simply stirring in more vinegar, or water or a combination thereof.

When first made this mustard harsh and unpleasant tasting, however after a day or two, it will still be quite hot but it mellows out to a wonderful rich flavor and is a wonderful condiment.

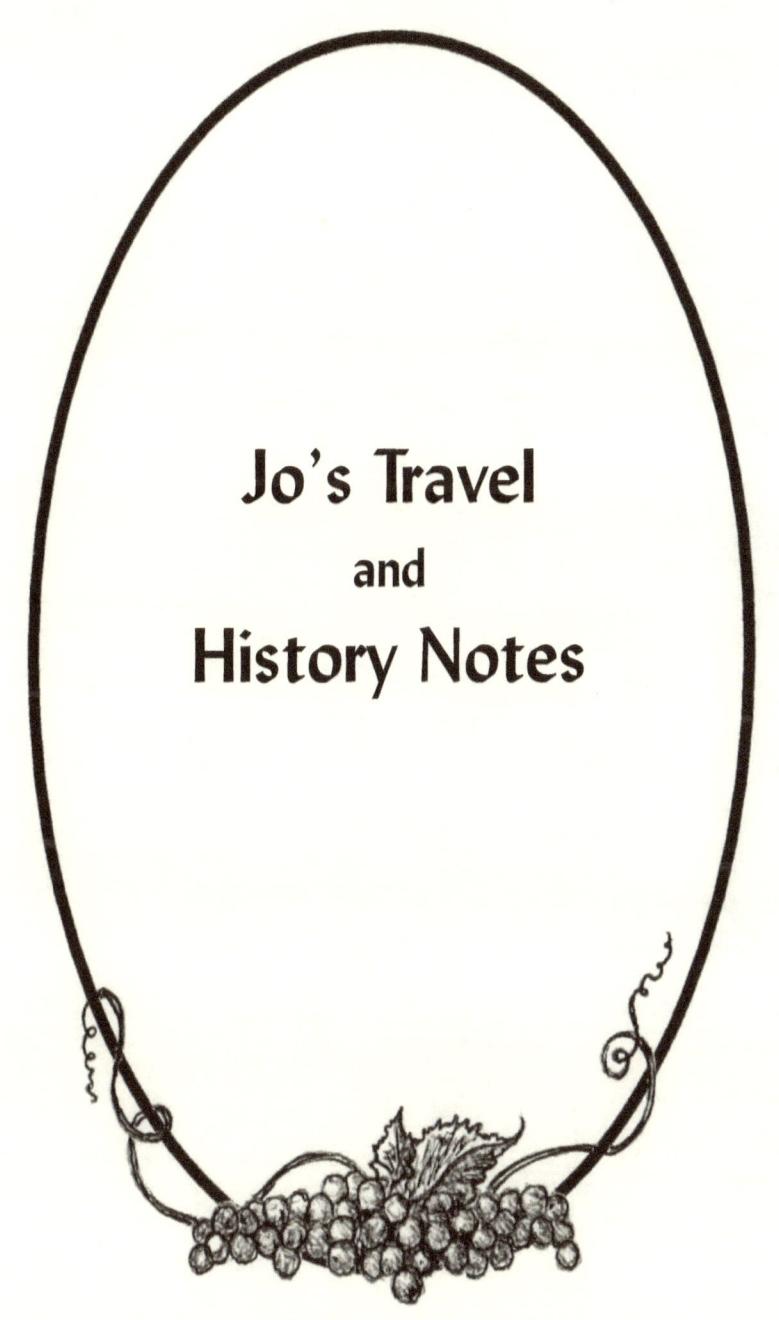

Jo's Travel

and

History Notes

Here are some notes I made during the period when this story takes place. Since I write travel material as well as cookbooks, I always have an eye out for interesting and out of the way places to visit, both at home and abroad. I am a tourist in my own back yard. I have always felt that if you don't find your own back yard interesting, you probably won't find much of interest anyplace else. If you live in Northern California and have never visited the University of California, what makes you think you will be uplifted by visiting Oxford? If you have never walked across the Golden Gate Bridge, why do you think you will be thrilled by going to the top of the Empire State Building? If you live in the Midwest and have never marveled at the majestic sweep of the prairie, why do you think you will be awestruck by the open grasslands of Africa or Argentina? There is something special and fascinating everyplace; well, perhaps not in Emeryville.

Josephine St. John

Some History Notes

My own fascination with history leads me to assume that everyone else is equally interested, so, here are notes about people and places that I find absolutely fascinating. If history bores the pants off you, well then, just don't read this part.

Gold: I have always thought it one of the greatest ironies in history, that the Spaniards, who came to the New World in search of gold, missed one of the greatest gold discoveries in history by a few miles and fewer years. They colonized up and down the coast, but never ventured east. They lost control of California when Mexico won her independence in 1822. In 1848, gold was discovered at Sutter's Mill, a mere 150 miles inland and twenty-six years later.

Los Californios refers to the mostly Mexican colonists who were awarded huge grants of land when Mexico gained her independence from Spain. Great ranching empires were created. Huge herds of cattle grazed the land. They were primarily used for tallow and hides. These ranchers were known as "Los Californios." Mariano Vallejo once said: "We were the pioneers of the Pacific coast, building towns and Missions while General Washington was carrying on the War of the Revolution. We often talk together of the days when a few hundred large ranches occupied the whole country from the Pacific to the San Joaquin."

These Rancheros enjoyed a leisurely lifestyle, which allowed them the time for family and tradition. Like in the American South in the days of the vast plantations, this utopian lifestyle was dependent on the labor of poor ranch hands and the virtual enslavement of the California Indians. Cowhides, called "California Banknotes," were used almost like currency. They were traded to Yankee trading-ship captains for the goods needed.

The Californios enjoyed a life of virtual independence, isolated as they were from whatever government was in power, be it Spain, Mexico or the United States. California was almost an island, being isolated by the Pacific Ocean to the west, a scorching desert to the south and the almost impenetrable Sierra Nevada to the East. This early independent mindset has had lasting impact on the personality of California and we Californians.

 **Mission San Francisco Solano,** (Sonoma Mission,) was the last and northernmost of the chain of twenty-one California Missions. It is the only mission founded after Mexico's independence from Spain. It was also the only mission founded without the approval of the Church. Founded in 1823, the first building was built of wood covered with whitewashed mud. The usual help in the form of supplies from other missions did not arrive. Help did come however, from friendly Russian fur traders who donated supplies and Russian-designed bells. By 1832 the mission sported substantial adobe buildings with tile roofs, arranges around a large square courtyard, including a twenty-seven room residence for the padres and guests of the missions, a church, storehouse and workshops. Outside the mission compound, there were orchards, vineyards, a gristmill, housing for soldiers, a jail, a cemetery and an infirmary. Over 10,000 acres of land were dedicated to agriculture. There were 5,000 sheep and 2,000 head of cattle as well as numerous crops. All this of course depended on the enforced labor of the local Indian population. Mission Sonoma became one of the most successful of all the missions. After secularization, the mission fell into gradual decline, much aided by the 1906 earthquake. Eventually the Historic Landmarks League purchased the mission property and with the help of state funds, began restoration. When completed, the League turned the property over to the state. The Mission is now part of Sonoma State Historic Park.

Don Mariano Guadalupe Vallejo served California under three flags; the Spanish, the Mexican and that of the United States. He was born a subject of Spain and was personal secretary to the Spanish governor of California when news of Mexico's independence reached Monterey. Under the flag of Mexico, he became Commander of the Presidio of San Francisco in 1833, and oversaw the secularization of Mission San Francisco Solano. In 1835 he was appointed Commandant and Director of Colonization of the Northern Frontier. He began construction of a presidio in Sonoma to forestall further colonization from the Russians who were already in Fort Ross. He had long been in favor of California joining the United States and although he was taken prisoner during the Bear Flag Revolt, after the Unites States defeated Mexico in the Mexican/American war, he became a staunch advocate, encouraging the Californios to accept American rule.

He was a rancher with vast holdings in and around Sonoma, including the Petaluma Adobe which was the center of his ranching operation. He was also one of the early vintners in Sonoma Valley. It was he who encouraged Agoston Haraszthy to move his wine making operations to Sonoma. Two of Vallejo's daughters married two of Haraszthy's sons in a double wedding in the chapel at the Sonoma Mission.

Hungarian **Agoston Haraszthy**, although never a complete financial success, was certainly an amazing man of many talents. He should be considered a true "Renaissance Man." He made his first trip to the United States in 1840 and fell in love the country and was determined to move here. Coming from a family of vintners, he was also convinced that someplace in this huge and wonderful land he would find the perfect place to grow grapes.

He first stopped in Sauk Prairie, Wisconsin and founded the oldest incorporated town in the state, Haraszthy Town which later became Sauk City. He also founded and operated the first steamboat line to engage in scheduled traffic on the upper Mississippi.

Due to his asthma, his doctor advised him to move to Florida or California. The discovery of gold decided him on California. He first settled in San Diego where he operated a livery stable, stage line, and butcher shop. He planted grapes but the venture was not successful. He became the first town marshal and the first county sheriff. This was because he built and owned the jail, built with bricks made in his brickyard, the first in California. The climate in San Diego became uncomfortable for him after he attempted to collect county taxes, so he moved to Northern California where he also attempted to plant grapes.

When the new U.S. Mint in San Francisco was established, he was appointed assayer. This was because he was a self taught metallurgist and developed a more efficient method of smelting the Placer Ore that was coming in from the Mother Lode. His method incidentally, is still used. Several years later, he was forced to resign and there was a grand jury investigation because far less gold was coming out of the building than was going in. He was charged with embezzling over $150,000.00. He was exonerated however, after someone noticed that the roofs surrounding the mint glittered. It was discovered that flakes of gold were escaping through the flue of the smelter and gilding the surrounding roofs.

In 1857 he met Vallejo and they became great friends. Vallejo invited him to visit Sonoma, and convinced him that is was the perfect place for his wine making endeavors. He purchased land just outside of town and named it Buena Vista (Beautiful View). Up to this time most wines in California were produced from the grape stock originally brought by the Mission Padres and the wines were less than remarkable. Haraszthy experimented with many new techniques and was able to improve on the existing methods but was still not satisfied. He convinced the State Legislature that California's future lay in agriculture, not gold, and was commissioned to travel to Europe to collect vine cuttings. He traveled through France, Germany, Italy, Switzerland and Spain and brought back over 100,000 cuttings of some 350 varieties, which became the foundation or California's premium wine industry. He also brought back cuttings for fruit trees which became the foundation for

California's citrus and prune industries. Yes, prunes. The prune industry in California was so large at one time that Californians were called "Prune Pickers."

In 1863 his sons Arpad and Attila married Vallejo's daughters Joveta and Natalia. Despite his brilliance and creativity, he was never a total financial success. As the result of an outbreak of phylloxera and a fire in the winery, his already fragile financial situation was sent into a tailspin and he filed for bankruptcy. He eventually moved to Nicaragua where he planned to develop a sugar plantation. One day he set out alone on a mule to investigate the progress of a new sawmill. He never returned home and no trace of him was ever found. It is believed that he tried to cross a river on a fallen log, lost his balance, fell into the water and was eaten by an alligator.

On the 100th anniversary of his death, Congress recognized his contributions with an entry in the official Congressional Record that said in part: "In a very significant way, Agoston Haraszthy put California on the nation's economic and gourmet maps..."

The Buena Vista Winery still exists and it still produces premium wines. The winery is well worth a visit. Agoston Haraszthy is considered to be the father of modern viniculture and the founder of the premium wine industry in California.

The Epic Campaign (End Poverty in California) refers to the 1934 gubernatorial election when liberal novelist, Upton Sinclair ran for governor of California on the Democratic ticket. Sinclair had been a lifelong advocate of the people and saw this as a way he could further his work in achieving social reforms. Conservative opposition, lead by the Hurst Newspaper conglomerate, joined forces behind his opponent, Frank F. Merriam and successfully defeated him in what remains one of the foremost examples of negative propaganda techniques in political history in the United States.

The Bear Flag Rebellion refers to a group of disgruntled Americans who, deciding to emulate the Texans, and revolted against Mexican rule in California. On June 14, 1846 under the leadership of U.S. Army Captain John C. Frémont, a group of men rode into the town of Sonoma, surrounded General Vallejo's home and held him prisoner. They proceeded to get rip-roaring drunk, raised a make shift flag with a bear and star on it and proclaimed California an Independent Republic. Unbeknownst to the men, war between Mexico and the United States had already been declared on May 13. The news took until mid-July to reach California.

The Republic lasted less than a month. In July, American forces landed in Monterey and overthrew the Mexican Coastguard troupes garrisoned there. The "Bear Flaggers" gave up their idea of an independent republic. Frémont and others rode south, surrendered the Bear Flag to the U.S. forces, and joined in the efforts to make California part of the United States. The original "Bear Flag," which served as a model for the official California State Flag, was destroyed in the 1906 San Francisco earthquake and fire.

Some Travel Notes

As an independent travel writer, I try to seek out points of interest that are often overlooked by the standard guidebooks. Here are some of my favorite places in and about the Historic town of Sonoma. Some are quite well known and some are hidden treasures.

 **The Town of Sonoma**, although a high tourist destination, nonetheless manages to retain a hometown feel. A walk around the plaza is a lesson in the history of architecture with buildings ranging from Mission era through Victorian. Many of the buildings are under the care of Sonoma Historic State Park and open to the public. Others are occupied by the usual assortment of businesses and eateries, catering to tourists; the range is from tourist-tacky to extremely nice. If you plan on putting together a wine country picnic you couldn't do better than to get your bread at the **Basque Boulangerie Café** on the Plaza on First Street. Unfortunately it's now a Yuppie cafe and espresso house, however, they still make the finest sourdough bread in the county, perhaps even in California. On the north side of the Plaza, Spain Street, you'll find the **Sonoma Cheese Factory**. They carry an excellent selection of cheeses, wines and other munchables, however, they are quite pricy and during the season, they're packed out with visitors. If you are adventurous, go just down the street to East Second Street to **Vella Cheese** or walk a little further to **The Cheese Maker's Daughter** on East Napa. Before leaving The Plaza, be sure to visit the **Mission**, the **Vallejo Barracks**, the **Tascano Hotel**, the **Swiss Hotel**, the **Blue Wing Inn** and the **Vasquez House**.

The Vasquez House was built in the early 1850's for General "fighting" Joe Hooker of Civil War Fame. He sold it and its surrounding acreage to the Vasquez family who lived there until 1901. It is located in a small court behind the Blue Wing Inn and accessed through a walkway at the side of La Casa Restaurant.

 **This Bell**, located where Broadway ends at the Plaza, marks the end of El Camino Real. The other end is at Mission San Diego. El Camino Real (the Kings highway) was a road up the coast of California, linking the twenty-one Missions, Pueblos and Presidios. These establishments were originally laid out to be one days ride apart, thus providing hostelries for travelers.

 **Lachryma Montis**, or tears of the mountain, is located just half a mile west of the Plaza on West Third Street. This was the home of General Vallejo and his family. It gives you an excellent insight into the lifestyle of the time. As part of the Sonoma State Historic Park system, it is open to the public.

 **The Old Mountain Cemetery** is nestled under Live-Oaks in the hills above town. The Vallejo, Sebastianies, some of the Harasztys, and many other early Sonoma residents are buried here. It's a beautiful cemetery and a good place for a quiet picnic.

 **Jack London State Historic Park** is about ten miles north of Sonoma, outside the town of Glen Ellen. Jack London did a lot more than write dog stories. He was a true Renaissance Man. He bought Beauty Ranch, the site of the park, with proceeds from his books, and planned to make it a model agricultural endeavor. He designed **Wolf House**, the ruins of which are still there. It was built with lava rock quarried on the ranch and redwood timbers milled there. Unfortunately Wolf House burned just a few days before the Londons were scheduled to move in. After Jack's death, his widow, Charmian London, built **The House of Happy Walls**, a classic example of Arts and Crafts architecture. It is now a memorial to Jack London and the repository for photographs and artifacts commemorating the life of this world-famous author and

197

social reformer. A short hike from the house you may visit the London's grave site. It's a beautiful place to sit and meditate. The park is open to the public and well worth a visit.

 **The Petaluma Adobe State Historic** Park is located on Adobe Road, about half way between Sonoma and Rohnert Park. More than just a park and museum, this is a living history facility. In addition to the exhibits depicting life during the Mission era, there are also costumed docents in period dress demonstrating various skills of the period. This is a particularly good place to visit with children.

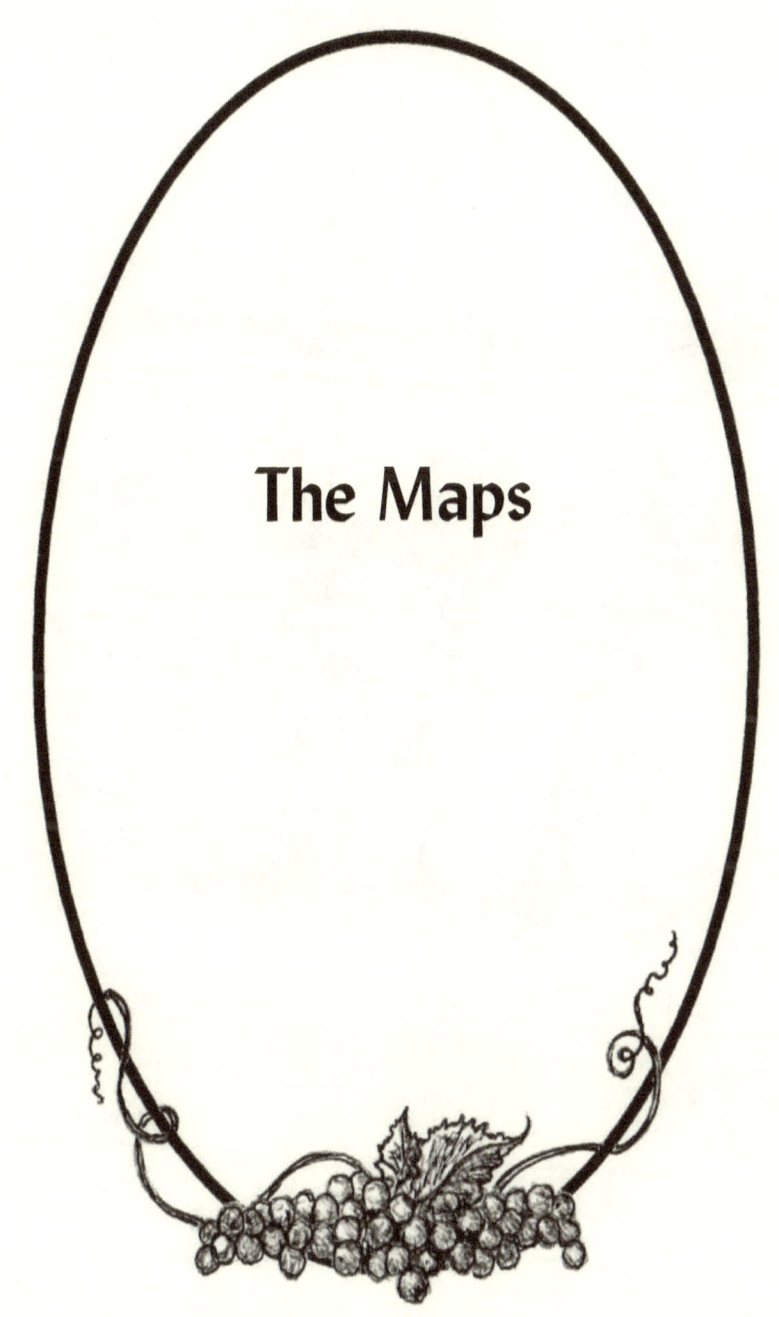

The Maps

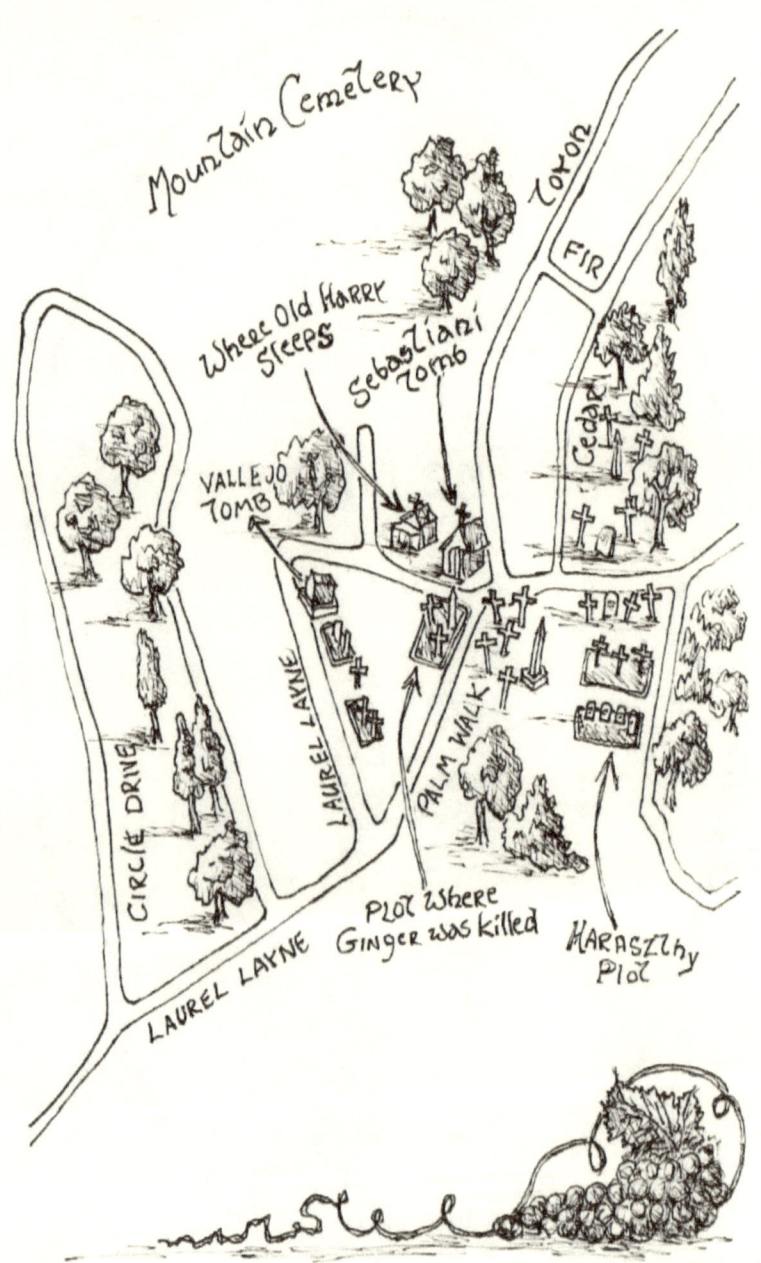

Mountain Cemetery

Toyon

FIR

Cedar

Where Old Harry Sleeps

Sebastiani Tomb

VALLEJO TOMB

LAUREL LAYNE

PALM WALK

CIRCLE DRIVE

LAUREL LAYNE

Plot Where Ginger was killed

HARASZThy Plot

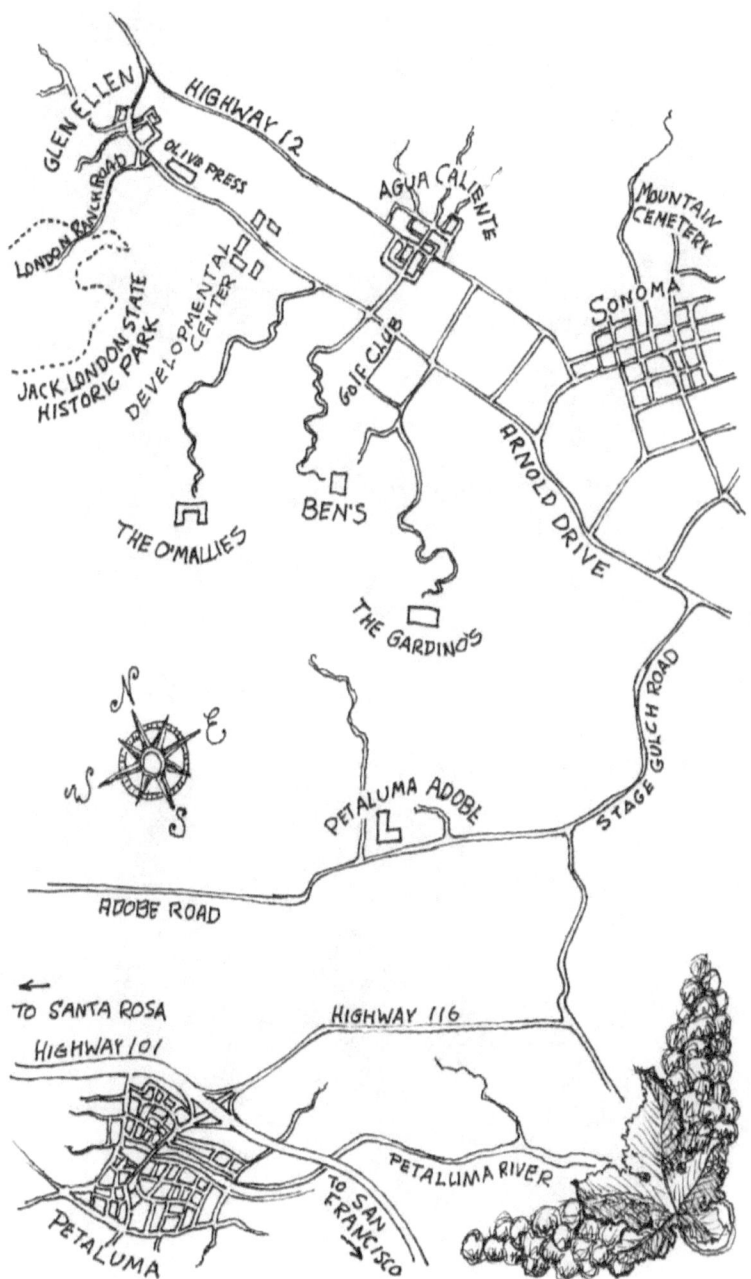

GLEN ELLEN

HIGHWAY 12

OLIVE PRESS

AGUA CALIENTE

London Ranch Road

MOUNTAIN CEMETERY

JACK LONDON STATE HISTORIC PARK

DEVELOPMENTAL CENTER

SONOMA

GOLF CLUB

THE O'MALLIES

BEN'S

THE GARDINOS

ARNOLD DRIVE

N
E
W
S

PETALUMA ADOBE

STAGE GULCH ROAD

ADOBE ROAD

TO SANTA ROSA

HIGHWAY 116

HIGHWAY 101

PETALUMA RIVER

TO SAN FRANCISCO

PETALUMA

201

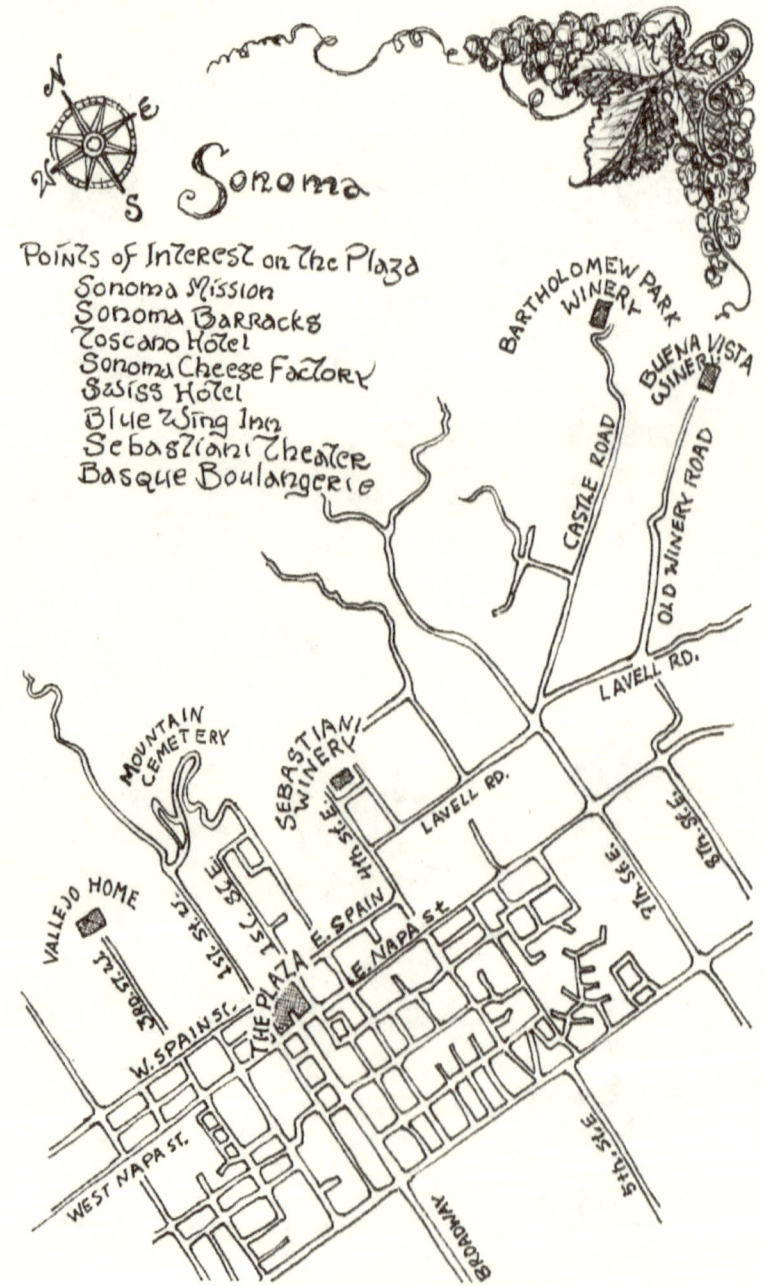

Sonoma

Points of Interest on The Plaza
    Sonoma Mission
    Sonoma Barracks
    Toscano Hotel
    Sonoma Cheese Factory
    Swiss Hotel
    Blue Wing Inn
    Sebastiani Theater
    Basque Boulangerie

BARTHOLOMEW PARK WINERY

BUENA VISTA WINERY

CASTLE ROAD

OLD WINERY ROAD

LAVELL RD.

MOUNTAIN CEMETERY

SEBASTIANI WINERY

LAVELL RD.

4TH ST. E.

7TH ST. E.

8TH ST. E.

VALLEJO HOME

1ST ST. E.

1ST ST. E.

BROADWAY

THE PLAZA

E. SPAIN

E. NAPA ST.

E. NAPA ST.

W. SPAIN ST.

WEST NAPA ST.

BROADWAY

5TH ST. E.

4TH ST. E.

203

Other Books by
Geraldine Duncann

The English
Country Kitchen

Geraldine Duncann

artichoke

extravaganza

GERALDINE DUNCANN

Cake Mix Classics
Sensational Treats Baked The _Easy_ Way

Geraldine Duncann

Retro
FIESTA

A Gringo's Guide to
Mexican Party Planning

Geraldine Duncann

A is for CODA-WADA

GERALDINE DUNCANN

absolutely
avocado

COOK WEST

GERALDINE DUNCANN

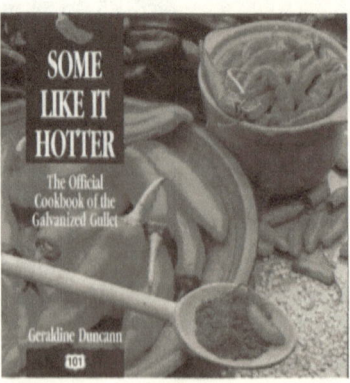

SOME
LIKE IT
HOTTER

The Official
Cookbook of the
Galvanized Gullet

Geraldine Duncann

101

About the Author

Food and travel writer
Geraldine Duncann,
is the author of numerous cookbooks, including
the best-selling, "Some Like it Hotter" and
"The English Country Kitchen." She has also published
a large number of travel articles. Her peregrinations have
taken her to many out-of-the-way places in her ongoing efforts
to seek out interesting recipes and the people who produce them.

She was educated at the California College of Arts and Crafts
in Oakland, California where she studied design, color,
composition and photography. She studied privately with such
noted artists as Jade Fon, Jonathon Bachelor, Richard Diebenkorn
and Antonio Prieta. After leaving Arts and Crafts she became
increasingly interested in writing, history, folk traditions and
the culinary arts, all of which led to her career as a food and
travel writer.

Geraldine is a fifth generation Californian, her great-great-
grandparents having arrived in the golden state shortly after
the gold rush. She lives in the heart of the Sonoma County
wine country, surrounded by some of the world's
most prestigious Zinfandel vineyards.